Contents

I0543197

Colophon

While the title says "autobiographies," these stories are works of fiction. If it sounds real, well, that's what a writer does.

While some of the names and places are real, what happens with them in these stories is not. I have used my official creative license (shown upon request) with people, history, time, space, and action.

A note about the fonts in the printed edition: The body copy is *PNM Caecilia* by Peter Matthias Noordzij https://www.teff-type.com. The cover type and headlines are in the wonderful free *Retro Signature* by Nirmana Visual. https://nirmanavisual.com/

Thanks!

To my friends and family—both biological and logical. You know who you are. I love and am grateful for you! (Especially the playful ones.)

I'd also like to thank the characters who told me their stories. Writing is about getting out of your own way and listening.

Cover and book design by the author.

You can blame him if you think the handwriting font is hard to read but he won't care—it's his book. Play your cards right and you can choose the fonts for your own book, too.

www.WILL-HARRIS.com

introduction

In my first therapy session, I said, "All I want is to understand everything." That's why I tell stories. To experience more than just *my* life.

Physically, we are limited to the senses of our body. But when we're open to the stories in the ether we can go anywhere, be anyone, and experience everything, even death and what comes after.

15 years ago I completely changed how I wrote. Like most people, I was taught to start with an idea, theme and structure. But on

that fateful day, I gave myself permission to *let the character tell the story.*

Most characters have the same five senses and emotions we do. With that in common we can feel and experience their world the same way they do.

Because I was inside the character I could experience what he saw, heard, smelled, tasted and touched—and how it made him feel. The story that emerged from that was full of surprising detail and emotion. I was so entranced that I told a new story every day on my walks.

That's where these stories started. I've been discovering them ever since.

Stories are all around us. When you get out of your own way you can experience them. You don't have to "make them up," they're out there, waiting to be found.

Stories are the only human creation that doesn't decay and disappear over time. Tales from 1000s of years ago can still be just as fresh and compelling today.

I love writing—and teaching others that they have the power to tell their own stories.

Writing gives you the power to discover the joy of walking in someone else's shoes and inhabit their senses and emotions. It lets you experience a world bigger than just your own.

Living inside other people gives us more empathy for others—and ourselves.

I hope that these short stories help you escape the confines of yourself for a little while. And that experiencing life through someone else's perspective might encourage you to discover stories of your own.

Now, on with the stories!

i

am

story

I have been waiting for you. Hoping you'd stop thinking long enough to listen.

That's what we want in this world—for somebody to see us and hear us—not through their own distorted prism of life, but through a pure lens, shaped by experiences but not clouded by them.

Flawless and unselfconscious, feeling my senses and emotions as clearly and unfiltered as they can be seen.

Seeing my world with wonder.

I don't have answers, I only have sights and smells and tastes and feelings. So many feelings.

Maybe that's where I come from. Maybe the feelings of an event or lifetime require too much energy to be held within one small brain, one small being.

Maybe as they explode out from us, they attach to the energy of the earth and the atmosphere where they can be free, yet always remaining what they were, preserved, intact, patient, yet still vibrating with energy.

If you're not careful you feel my stories anyway, from strangers on the street, on the bus, in the restaurant, the next car, or next to you in bed. From people you work with, love, or have never met. They infect you, unconsciously.

You wonder why you suddenly feel so sad, or angry. You *can't figure out* the reason. You *can't think your way out of emotions.*

You can only feel your way.

But instead of feeling, you tune out, turn on the TV or Radio or Internet.

You try to avoid the square rawness that has yet to be polished, cleanly, to fit in your round holes.

But there's a better way. You don't have to react against the roughness, fight the feeling, and ignore the unknown.

Instead, you can start to feel it for what it is:

A *human story.*

That's the reason we're on this planet for this time. So that we can create these experiences, these memories, this energy— that powers something in the universe we don't yet understand.

So listen.

Without judgments, *without* that hazy prism of ego you think of as *you.*

Allow the story to reach *through* you, to permeate and percolate and produce something new that came *not out of you, but through you.*

Unafraid to let it affect you, change you, and expand you. Because that's the best thing that can happen.

Martin in the Mangroves

"Martin in the Mangroves" was my favorite story as a kid. Partly because my name is Marty, but also because of the word "mangrove."

Of course, I didn't know at the time it would have significant meaning to me, but I could imagine these groves of men and it was kind of thrilling and terrifying at the same time.

The story was about a boy named Martin (I saw myself as the boy), who gets thrown overboard from a pirate ship in a storm.

His father was The Pirate Frederick. I don't know why but you can stick the word "pirate" in front of anything and it sounds more exciting. So whenever I met anybody named "Fred" I'd wonder if they were a pirate.

Obviously I had a vivid if not overactive imagination.

So in the story, Martin is thrown overboard during a storm. He's starting to drown and he sees what he thinks is a merman, a male mermaid.

But the merman turns out to be a manatee. Now, Martin lost his glasses in the storm, which can explain his confusion, because otherwise it seems like it would be hard to confuse the two. But when you're reading the book and you see the illustrations, it was one very handsome manatee.

So the manatee carries Martin on his back to the mangroves where he lives. I must admit, at first, I was a little bit disappointed that the mangroves didn't actually consist of men somehow growing out of the swamp, because when I heard the word that's what I thought it was.

But it was this dark and mysterious place from which many magical things happened. One of the magical things was that Martin discovered that the manatee's name was also Martin.

So, clearly, all this was fated to happen, right? Martin, the manatee, had a great sense of humor—he could communicate with the human Martin just through bubbles.

They'd blow bubbles underwater and they'd totally understand what the other was saying.

Then, of course, I'd get in a pool and blow bubbles and try to get my sister Anna to understand what I was saying and she would say I was farting and yell at me.

But it was still a wonderful idea.

One of the key things that happen in the story is that the Martins deeply love each other. When I was a kid I thought it was brotherly love, and I never had a brother. So that was another great thing about the story, because I thought, "Oh, if I had a brother, better yet, a twin..." and the story even suggests that in a magical way the two Martins are twins, even soulmates of different species.

The exact wording in the book is... let me see what page, page 126, I marked the corner so it's easy to find because it's one of my favorite passages, it says, "The Martins," (he called both of them together 'The Martins') "would swim together for hours, blowing bubbles and sharing their deepest secrets. It was as if the two of them had been formed as twins, yet separated by some cosmic storm and given birth on different sides of the sea."

I loved that idea—they were one egg that split, with one carried by currents across the sea.

I loved it because I secretly hoped I wasn't really my father's son. Maybe I'd somehow been sent across the sea by mistake, you know what I mean? And that I was going to find my true soulmate, my other Martin.

When I think about it now, it's all kind of prophetic, and weird, but weird in that wonderful way that the world sometimes works.

Then what happens in the story is the Pirate Frederick is sailing near the mangroves and he sees Martin, his son, or at least the boy he raised, riding on the back of the manatee, as if he's surfing across the middle of the sea.

Pirate Frederick doesn't think it's his son, he thinks it's a ghost or a demon, because number one, his son would certainly have drowned in that storm, and two, no human boy could do this!

It didn't help that Pirate Frederick drank a lot and had pretty much lost his mind when Martin fell overboard.

So then, and this is a really awful, awful scene, you see Pirate Frederick on the ship preparing a harpoon, because as well as being pirates they were also whalers.

He's preparing the harpoon to kill the demon he thinks his son is.

Not only is it a horrible image, it's how I felt as a child, too, because I knew my father didn't like me. He never liked me. He would say things like, "Why can't you be like a *normal* boy?" and other things I've blocked out of my head because I didn't want to hear them.

I didn't know how to be a normal boy. I only knew how to be a boy who read books and lived in my imagination and wanted to stay inside instead of going out and playing ball like my father had.

Every time he said those things it was as if he was loading a harpoon and shooting it straight into my heart.

That's exactly what the Pirate Frederick was doing with his Martin.

There's this scary section, let me open it, page 262, where you see the harpoon being shot, then for the next five pages, there's nothing but drawings of the harpoon speeding through midair.

Then on page 267 you see Martin joyously riding the manatee, and you know what's coming.

Every time I read that story, and I read it hundreds of times, I would be yelling at the book... another reason my father probably thought I wasn't a normal child. I'd yell at the book hoping Martin would hear me and that the story would somehow magically change.

But it never did.

It was always the same.

The harpoon entered page 268.

Only now it was diving towards the water, and instead of hitting Martin the boy, it hit Martin the manatee.

It never failed, every time I read it, and even now remembering the story, I cry because it was like half of Martin was killed by his father.

The manatee let out a piteous cry. Martin the boy knew what happened and held onto his friend even as they sank under the water, deeper and deeper.

Meanwhile, Pirate Frederick thought he'd been successful in scaring away the demon, but, in fact, he was killing his own son.

The boy sank deeper and deeper in the water, clutching onto his manatee, unwilling to let him go.

The surface got farther away. The light was fading.

Many times when I read the story I would stop reading right here. In fact, the first copy of the book I had, I tore out the last few pages, I didn't want to read the rest of the story.

In my imagination, the harpoon would only make a flesh wound. When the boy removed the harpoon they could both swim back to the surface—up to Pirate Fredrick where they could say, "We are real, we are normal. Please love us!"

In my version of the story, the Pirate Fredrick takes them both in the boat, even the manatee, and the boy grows up to be the kind of pirate that would never harpoon anything or anybody.

He's kind to all the fish and dolphins and whales so he becomes king of the sea...

But in the book version, the manatee is mortally wounded. With his dying bubbles, he tells the boy to save himself.

But the boy will not let go. So the manatee uses his last bit of life to shake off the boy and with one powerful push of his flipper, sends him towards the surface.

Then with one final puff of bubbles, the manatee says, "We will always be together in your heart."

Martin emerges from the waves, tears streaming down his face, tears as salty as the sea, and he looks up and there's the pirate ship and his father.

The Pirate Frederick reaches down, pulls Martin onto the ship, and welcomes him back with open arms. His boy. His son.

Martin goes on to be a pirate himself. A strong man—who has learned that the greatest strength is kindness.

Then in one very short closing chapter, just one paragraph, the boy, now a man, sails the seven seas and never stops looking for his manatee.

So excuse me for a minute while I cry, because I hate that ending, I hate it.

There I was, this little kid, basically thinking that life is hopeless. That you'll find the person who you feel the closest to in the world, that you will love the most, then they will die by having your father kill them.

And my entire life was colored by this notion. I was afraid to love anybody, especially the ones I wanted to love the most because what would that mean? It would mean I was dooming them—killing them with my love.

Obviously I could never tell my father I was gay. It would just confirm his worst fears about how I was never a normal boy.

When I was 28, my father died in a boating accident. He'd always loved to sail, I thought that's why he gave me the book, but maybe it was something else.

He was sailing and there was a sudden storm and he simply disappeared.

I was horribly sad and terribly relieved. I hoped that somewhere, under the water, there was a manatee that would love him.

And that there was one waiting for me, too.

Cristobal

I watched him, watching me. Every day I took this walk back from the dress shop, and every day he followed me. He didn't know that I knew he was there.

I wondered why he stared at me—at first I thought it was my dresses, elegant and fine, unlike what the peasant women wore in this town. There were other women of means here, that's who I sold my dresses to, but they didn't live in this part of town—Costa Bahía, the bay side, where I grew up.

It became a ritual, him following me. I was not frightened, back then boys were not hooligans, they were like little animals, waiting to turn, unfortunately, into men.

I had been a failure at childbirth, twice, so it was natural that my husband took a mistress who bore two children for him—both boys. They were illegitimate, of course, but he talked about adopting them to take over his legacy. Why should I mind, he had taken care of me.

I bought a small house with a view of Porto Mañana, and was quite happy there by myself with my servant girl, Maria.

I designed and made dresses, bought them from Paris, too. Not for income, but for something artistic to do. I loved the feel of silk shantung against my fingertips, the cold steel needle warming in my hand, pushing the thread through the fabric, tightening, turning two pieces into one. I could make something beautiful.

It was a drizzly March afternoon—the kind where everything looks shiny, but sad—when the boy was close enough for me to see his eyes. Dark, curious, looking me straight in the eye, something even grown men could rarely do.

It was the way he looked at *me*, not just my body, that made me call out to him, "Chico!" a local affectionate term for a boy. I hadn't meant for it to sound like the kind of order I give to Maria or one of my sewing assistants, but that's how it came out.

He seemed as if he was going to run away, but he stopped and turned. Then he walked slowly, tentatively, towards me. I realized he'd grown since he started following me, and now he was a handsome young man, maybe 16 or 18, I didn't know these things.

He had a fine figure I could see because his clothes were a little too small. I liked the way his collar was worn, frayed almost into a fringe. I would use that.

I knew he would not speak first—that would be impolite to a woman, especially one of higher stature. So I spoke.

"Why do you follow me?" I asked, as kindly as I could, not wanting to scare him.

"Beautiful lady," he started, his voice still young but like a man. "I only wish to gaze upon you." I gasped a little, feeling the cool air in my nostrils, making me feel lightheaded.

He had the kind of old-fashioned speech of the peasants, something I found charming and honest, after the affected speech of the women in my circles, practiced in Paris, every word carefully uttered so as not to sound like... a peasant, which many of them, like me, had been.

"You look cold," I said when I saw him shiver.

"No, it is seeing your beauty this close," he said, in a way that so surprised me. I could tell from his face he meant it—but he was a boy and I was a married woman of 38, old enough to be his mother.

I didn't know what to say. He had given me such an extraordinary gift with his words that I wanted to thank him. "I have paella on the stove if you are hungry."

"I can take care of myself," he said, with the pride of a man.

"I know you can, I would like to give you something for your kindness."

His skin was dark but I could still see him blush.

"I love paella," he said.

And then he did something unexpected—shocking—he reached out his hand to me—and I shocked myself—I took it.

We walked that way, hand-in-hand, down the cold, wet streets to my house. Along the way I wondered what he was thinking—was I a mama to him? A friend?

His hand was so warm that the cold went away. I heard our footsteps and his breathing and almost passed my own door, even though I'd painted it red in a sea of black doors.

#66, the brass letters were shiny because Maria polished them every day. They were a folly—a bit of jewelry on my front door.

Something that made me smile every time I saw their shell-like curves.

Maria had heard me coming and was already at the door. She looked at me like I had picked up a mangy dog from the street.

"Maria, we have a guest for dinner." I said, quickly, not meaning to put her in her place but to make sure she treated... I didn't yet know his name... as a guest.

Maria nodded but kept looking at the boy—he glanced at her but rarely took his eyes off me.

We went inside where it was warm. I removed my cape and he took it from me, hanging it gently on the mirrored stand near the door. The cape was a crisp black waxed cotton—elegant only in its simplicity. But today I was wearing a ruby silk charmeuse dress of the New Look, and the color instantly made the black and white hallway glow.

He did not have a coat and he was wet. I didn't know where he would be able to sit.

"Wait for me here for a moment..." I paused.

"Cristobal," he said, quietly.

I knew the name, it was very old. It meant, "Beautiful Christian," and in this light, he was beautiful, indeed.

I was aware of the rustle of my skirt as I went up the stairs, looking down to see him, unmoving, looking up at me.

I went into my nighttime closet—I knew I had something—for a former lover... oh, well, it was for a man anyway.

I had made a black silk robe, with gold trim for Hector. He had been a matador in his earlier years and still had a commanding presence. But his injuries took their toll, and he was run down by a bus while visiting his daughter in Seville.

I kept the robe, I even thought about selling them at my shop but then thought better of it, knowing that women will talk and they would assume... It wasn't as if they were angels, themselves, they whispered many secrets during our fittings... but still, to the outside world, we women still had to seem like perfect Madonnas.

I placed the robe over my arm, along with a Turkish towel, and walked down the stairs, trying not to make noise with my skirt because I found it embarrassing.

Cristobal was still standing there, but I caught him looking at the room, then me.

"Everything around you is of beauty," he said, as if he were in church, and I felt this wave of... was it happiness... joy, yes, it was joy— at his appreciation of things I had long ago stopped seeing myself.

Suddenly the simple chandelier was, indeed, as beautiful as the day I chose it in Madrid.

"Thank you. You may go into the library, dry yourself, and change into this," I said, handing the robe and towel to him.

He looked embarrassed himself.

"It's perfectly fine," I assured him, "Maria will dry your clothes on the stove."

"Of course, I do not want my clothes to soil your furniture," he said, simply, taking the items so gently I almost did not feel them leave my arm.

I closed the pocket doors behind him to give him privacy, and then in a shameful moment, I almost peered through the crack— I wanted to see him. But I did not.

I thought about his words. "my clothes to soil…" he said. So he knew it wasn't about *him*.

As I heard him approaching the doors I moved away—I did not want him to think I had been looking—but how I wished I had— and he slid the doors open.

His hair was tousled from the towel, shining, and while this robe was a little long for him (I could hem it), he emerged a different creature entirely. Like Neptune's child, fresh from the sea into a new world.

"Thank you," he said, pulling his belt tighter, "I have never felt anything like this… I have no words."

Another thing I took for granted in a world of wool and cotton, silk was always the thing closest to my skin—like a cool breeze and a warm hand.

He reached out his hand again and this time I dare not touch it—I gestured to the dining room and said, "This way, please."

He followed me into the dining room with its red and gold brocade walls. How many times had I dined there alone?

I gestured to the gilded chair opposite mine, but he pulled out my chair and waited for me to sit.

I felt the hair on the back of my neck rise. Why did this country boy have such fine manners? Was he not what he seemed? Had I invited a burglar or gigolo into my home?

But when I looked into his face, I could see nothing but good.

Maria entered with the paella tureen, and once again she and Cristobal exchanged looks.

I ladled it into his bowl first, then mine. He waited for me to take the first bite. I did. I handed him a piece of bread, "It's a bit too salty," I said, apologetically.

He dipped his bread into it—he would have eaten this all his life, it was nothing new— the only difference was a hint of saffron in the rice, something the peasants couldn't afford.

"Delicious," he said, waiting for me to take another bite.

"Please feel free to eat," I told him, hoping he might stop looking at me for a moment. The room felt too warm.

Now it was my turn to watch him—as he ate, greedily, he must have been terribly hungry. Without his asking I ladled more from the tureen into his bowl. He looked up, for a moment like a grateful dog, then went back to the food.

"What is this special flavor in the rice?" he asked.

"It's saffron," I explained, "From the south."

"I have never tasted this. Thank you for your kindness."

I felt ashamed again, I had done nothing but invite a young man to dinner... and had thoughts about him that were... ridiculous... obscene, even. He was a boy... a beautiful young man...

"It is my pleasure," I said—honestly, using the local phrase for it rather than the one the rich ladies would have used which really meant nothing.

He put down his spoon and smiled.

"I made Natillas de Avellanas," I said, looking forward to the hazelnut custard myself. I had made it this morning with my own hands—I enjoyed cooking, but also enjoyed not having to do it every day.

"You made it? You make dresses, too."

"Yes, I make dresses, and I enjoy cooking." I was not making clever conversation because I didn't know what to say. Now I did not want dessert, I wanted to feel the boy's hand in mine again. But how? Maria was here. If I sent her home early there might be talk. It was one thing with Hector, a man of my own age, but with a boy?

I did only want to hold his hand—that's all. Even though his hands were rough, there was such a sweetness about him.

Maria brought the Natillas and whispered to me, "Ma'am, might I be excused early this evening, Consolata is not well."

I nodded at Cristobal then went into the kitchen with Maria. "I'm so sorry about your daughter," I said, pressing a 100 peseta coin into her hand, "In case you need medicine."

Maria was a good young woman. I appreciated her presence and care and sometimes felt guilty when I thought it was at the expense of her own family. I bought them gifts, and even made them clothes, but she was always my servant, and I was always her mistress.

"Be careful of the boy," she whispered.

I was alarmed.

"Why? What do you know?"

"He is the son of a fisherman, I have bought shrimp from him. I see the way he looks at you."

I patted her shoulder, "Thank you, Maria, I will take care."

She looked wary, as if she knew something I didn't. But I also didn't care. She left into the night, and I was alone... with him.

I entered the dining room and Cristobal was out of his chair, looking at a painting of ships in the bay. It had been painted 20 years ago, in 1880, by my beau at the time, Rodrigo. He moved to Paris to be a painter, and left me here.

Shortly after I met Ezequiel. I was beautiful. He was rich. This is how things are. I thought I loved him. I loved the silk.

"It was painted by a young man I knew at the time," I said. He was startled.

"It is deep. Like you." he said—guileless. That's what was so beguiling.

He looked into my eyes from across the room.

"What do you want, Cristobal?" It was the first time I said his name, and it made everything feel real.

"Just to be in your presence." he sighed. Oh, no, it was too sweet, too flattering, too...

"Perhaps to touch your hand once more." he smiled just a little bit.

No—he is too young, I thought, and just then he moved towards me—and I stood still. He reached out his hand—all the while looking into my eyes—and I took his hand.

He led me into the hallway, then up the stairs, and I followed, unable to resist.

He was careful removing my dress, but otherwise clumsy, as if he'd never done this before, but that was sweet. It didn't last long, he was young, but unlike grown men, he didn't fall asleep, he simply held me and looked into my eyes.

I knew this would never happen again. So I felt his warmth, and smelled the sea on his skin. I felt alternately foolish and girlish, and finally, when his eyes fluttered closed, and his breathing sounded like a puppy, I felt sleepy, too, and drifted off.

In the morning he was still there—it was too warm and we were a bit stuck to each other. But he was even more beautiful with the morning light across his face. Peasant stock, yes, but, perhaps like me, with a hint of nobility. A strong nose. Lips that reminded me of mountain ranges. And that sweet smile.

"Buenos días, tesoro," he whispered. He called me a "treasure," again an old term—but how beautiful.

"Buenos días, amante." It seemed too intimate to call him my lover, but we were, at least for a night, so I said it.

"I can cook, too," he said, apropos of nothing. "I will make you an omelette," he said, with pride.

No, Maria mustn't see him… but it was Sunday—she would not come in today. He kissed me on the cheek, then jumped out of bed gesturing towards the robe, "I do not want to soil it," he said, walking naked from the room.

This I wanted to see. I put on my own robe and followed him, watching him. When he reached the bottom of the stairs he looked up and smiled, unashamed.

I followed him into the kitchen and he looked around, finding a pan, the eggs, butter, an onion and potato. He sliced the potato and onion very fast and very thin and put them in the pan with butter, then he shook the pan.

"I worked in a restaurant when I was a boy," he said, as if he wasn't still. But, no, he wasn't. He was a *young* man, but a man.

He moved beautifully, even the way he scrambled the eggs and poured them into the hot pan with a flourish.

"I like making things," he said, as he slid the omelette perfectly out of the plan onto a waiting platter.

I had set the table, and we sat at it—me in my pink silk robe, and him in his birthday suit! It was an utterly delightful repast.

He was so comfortable in his own skin—and so animated this morning.

I took a bite. "This is delicious—like you," I said, blushing.

"I want to be like you," he said, startling me before he continued, "I want to make beautiful things. I don't like fishing—the fish are beautiful but I am not making them, I am just taking them. I like cooking—but I make, then it is gone..." he said as I took my last bite of the utterly delicious omelet.

"What do you want to make?" I asked him. Maybe I could help him in some small way.

"Dresses."

I pretended to chew even though there was nothing in my mouth, simply because I didn't want to have to speak, not knowing what to say. I knew many men who made dresses, but none of them loved women in... how do I say this… in the way a woman wants to be loved. Women feel beautiful in what they make, and feel comfortable around these men, but they are not lovers.

I felt stupid. So this is why the boy was following me. He did not care about me, just about my dresses. Then why did he take me to bed? Did he think it was necessary? It was not, but now I would feel uncomfortable with him as an apprentice…

"Why?" was all I could ask.

"I love my mama. She would make all our clothes and showed me how. I know what I was wearing was dirty, but I made it myself. I like making things that last—things that make people happy—and beautiful."

That was sincere enough but I still felt foolish.

"I may know of somewhere in Barcelona where you could apprentice," I said, somewhat coldly now, feeling as if I had been used. Not entirely used—I enjoyed it.

"I have dreamed of learning from you, my beauty."

Flattery, again! And again, so sweet and sincere.

"I did not approach you, my lady. I would never have done so. You called me. I have loved you for so long..." he stopped and blushed deeply, looking down and seeing his nakedness.

Once again I felt foolish, but in a wonderful, girlish way.

I reached out my hand to him and he took it lightly.

"We will start today."

Was he a boy or a man? A gigolo or couturier in the making? I did not know. I did not care.

We arrived at my shop early, no one else there.

"May I show you what I can do?" he asked, touching a bolt of dark blue cotton I normally used only to stiffen linings. "I will make myself new clothes so I do not soil anything here."

He pulled the bolt and I showed him to the work table. As in the kitchen, he worked quickly and sure—as if he knew this pattern by heart. The sound of the shears cutting through the fabric sounded different in his hands.

"May I use the machine?" He asked. I was surprised he knew how to use a sewing machine. Peasants usually made everything by hand, which is why they could be taught to make couture.

"Of course," I replied.

"I can sew by hand but it is slow. I learned the machine on the fishing boats."

I heard the bell at the door—we had only been there for an hour or two, but he was already sewing the buttons on his shirt. What had been a lining material looked crisp and handsome on him—almost military, but light.

I tended to Mrs. Torres, who had been waiting for a hat from Paris. I sold hats mostly because then the woman would also require a matching coat or dress, and she did. We discussed a cherry print I had just received from Rome, it would be darling on her. I only ever gave women what would look good on them, which is why I had an excellent reputation.

When she left I went into the back room, where Cristobal had rearranged fabric by color, like a rainbow on the wall.

I looked at him, handsome in his uniform, but something had changed.

His collar—was frayed into a fringe.

I swallowed and blinked, not wanting to cry. The boy was an artist.

The Bear

"**N**o officer, I don't know why you pulled me over."

That's what they all say. Liars. What do they think, if they act all innocent I'll hand 'em a rose and say, "Oh, that's OK, just don't do it again?"

Of course they know, they knew when they were doing it and thought they could get away with it. Some even get a thrill knowing it's wrong and thinking nobody will catch 'em. But I catch 'em and I don't let 'em off easy.

'Cause this is my job. To stop miscreants and make the world a safer place. Wanted to be a cop since I was a kid, like Superman—truth, justice and the American way, that's what I'm about.

So this sack of shit is trying to look all innocent and sweating at the same time. Innocent my ass.

"You crossed a double yellow line, *sir*." I always say "sir" or "ma'am" even though I'm thinking, "Dumb-ass Motherfucker."

"But I was turning left into a driveway... sir, officer." Oh, look, he remembered to call me officer. Innocent, yeah right.

I don't stop innocent people. I know what he was doing.

"You're telling me you didn't see the pedestrian?" I asked, leading him on. I know we're not supposed to lead them on but it's fun.

"No, sir... officer, I didn't see a pedestrian."

Yeah, so there was no pedestrian, but even so, the little snot didn't see it, so that just proves my point.

"Then you could have killed her, couldn't you? Because you were talking on your cell phone or texting your nanny or some other bullshit." I hate cell phones and I hate people who use 'em. Steve Jobs should have been shot but he's dead so nothing you can do about it now.

"No, my phone's in my pocket, I'll show..."

I felt for my gun. "Keep your hands down, sir."

This is what they do, the criminal minds, make up shit about getting their phone or wallet and then pull out a gun and kill an innocent policeman, leaving his kids orphans. My little girl... My ex-wife would miss the alimony, and, what the fuck is he trying to do now?

My stun gun was at his forehead level. "Leave your hands right where they are, do not move."

Oh, shit, now he's gonna cry. Jesus H Christ on a fucking cracker, I hate that pussy shit. Boys these days think it's all manly to cry. Bull fucking shit. He's gonna call his mama from jail and cry on her shoulder.

"Put your hands on the top of your head. Get out of the car and lie *face down* on the sidewalk."

I opened his door with one hand, keeping the gun on him with the other. This was a dangerous transition when he could reach in his pocket or kick me with a knife in his shoe. That's why I've taken Taekwondo all these years to thwart menaces to society like this.

"Don't try anything, fucktard," I said, because now he'd gone too far and I wasn't about to call this piece of shit "sir" anymore.

"Move slowly, any fast moves and I'll stun you." We're not allowed to point our regular guns at motorists anymore, at least I'm not. Bullshit order from the pansy chief after some old lady complained. Bitch.

These people need to realize that we are trying to help them, to help society. But no, they think we're "out to get them" or some crap. They have no idea how hard my job is or how seriously I take my vow to protect the public.

You are fucking kidding me—flip flops? It's 45 degrees out and drizzling and this little idiot is wearing flip flops? And jeans, of course jeans, always jeans, can't get these pricks into a real pair of pants because then they might have to get a job. The back of his t-shirt says, "Real men do it with a pick." Do what with a pick? He's no miner, I can tell you that.

"Hands on the top of your head and do not move or you'll get 50,000 volts through your loser body, piss and shit yourself and nobody but me will find it funny."

One hand holding the stun gun, pointed at his crotch—where it'll hurt the most, and the other getting his wallet out of his back pocket. Black nylon with velcro, I could have bet you money that's what this punk would have. Some kind of skater backpacker asshole, tromping all over mother nature and acting like he's doing the world a fucking favor.

The velcro's worn out and doesn't make a noise when I open the wallet and look for his license. What is all this shit, it's the size of a fucking brick and filled with little scraps of paper. Oh my fucking Christ, they're all fortunes from fortune cookies.

Probably hooked up with the Chinese mob or something. See how I'm putting my life on the line stopping known criminals with ties to the underworld, no thought of my own safety. Think about that next time I pull you over, fuckers.

There's his license, Christopher James. Two first names. Probably a faggot. I'm slipping, I should have known it from the Subaru he was driving, a known lesbian vehicle. He's like a male lesbian—a lesbiman! Sometimes I crack myself up.

Age 28, address, 516 Pinecone Lane, nice neighborhood, I can't afford a house there. Must be his parents. And look, he's an organ donor, how sweet, now I'll have to be nice to him.

I lean over close to his face and scream "WHO ARE YOUR CHINESE MOB CONNECTIONS?"

The little shit looks surprised—got him! Maybe I'll take down the entire ring.

One of the fortune cookie things has stuck to my thumb where I had some glue from trying to take the price tag off a new air freshener for the car. What does it say?

"Trust that tomorrow will come." Oh Jesus I hate these fucking things, of course tomorrow will come. What's on the other side in red? Numbers, fucking lotto numbers. Holy Christ these people are superstitious—unless—maybe this is some kind of code sending messages to international agents.

They ship the cookies overseas, unsuspected, full of hidden messages.

"Please officer, I'm cold." the punk says. Yeah, it's drizzling and yeah the ground's wet, but maybe if he was wearing real fucking shoes he wouldn't be complaining like a little bitch.

"And I'm required to follow procedure and do my job so if you move I will have to stun you and you will lose all feeling in your balls for the next 48 hours." I explain nicely, because I don't have to tell him that.

"Mr. James, if that's your real name, you have the right to remain silent..." I start.

"Officer, are you charging me with something?" he asks—moving no other muscle than his jaw—which tells me he's a trained agent of some kind.

"I don't have to charge you with anything to read you your rights, punk. Merely suspect you, and I suspect you."

"I'm really sorry, officer, I really am, I was just going to…"

"Shut up, let me finish reading your rights." And I read them, "Knowing and understanding your rights as I have explained them to you, are you willing to answer my questions without an attorney present?"

"Sir, I was going to my daughter's birthday, she turned 4 today, please sir."

That was a new one. They always said they were on their way to the hospital or mother's deathbed or something, never heard of a birthday party, way too trivial.

"She's at my sister's house because my wife died…"

Oh, there we go, probably gonna say he's on the way to her funeral—in fucking flip flops!

"in a plane crash in China going to pick up our daughter."

Another new one. What kind of sick mind would make up something like that?

Oh, crap, I'm tired of all this shit, and just tired. My feet hurt, these damned new boots have never fit right. The doc said that prednisone would make me feel bad.

"What's your daughter's name?" I ask—this will make or break it for this asshole. If he says "Ling Ling" he can say 'goodbye' to his balls."

"Tammy. That was her mother's name. Well, my wife's."

And I think of my ex-wife, Tandy, and our little girl... we were going to name her Marie but she never... would have been about this guy's age... nothing was ever the same after that. Holy mother of crap my eyes are getting teary... fucking prednisone, makes no fucking sense.

I can't do this anymore, I just can't. Let the world go to hell. Let the Chinese Mafia do whatever they're doing. And let this guy go home to his little girl... the little girl I might have had.

"I'm sorry, sir," is all I can get out without sounding like a total pussy. "I'm so very sorry," and now I can't stop it, I'm crying. I'm gonna get kicked off the force for this, a cop crying, Jesus fucking Christ.

"Get up—you can get up," I say, knowing he's not going to shoot me, not sure why I ever thought he would, he seems like a nice guy.

I see him crying and he sees me crying and we both start bawling like babies.

I'd never cried for Marie, never. That's why Tandy left. She told me, "You're a cold-hearted bastard who can't even cry for our daughter." But I loved her, and never stopped thinking what she might be like now, going to college, or... adopting a Chinese baby.

I hadn't cried in 22 years, not once, not over anything, even when I was shot and it just missed my spine, not even then. Not when I had to spend 6 months learning to walk again. Not when I finally got to go back home and there was nobody there. Not once.

And now I was sitting on a curb with my head in my hands, some stranger in a T-shirt patting me on the back.

"I'm sorry you've had such a hard day," he said to me. He was apologizing to me.

"What did you get her?" I ask. "for her birthday."

"I was on my way to buy a teddy bear," he said—and it was like *he'd* stunned *me*.

When Marie would have been two, I bought her a teddy bear. I went to the toy store and bought it and put it in the trunk of my car. Always kept it with me. Kept in a SDPD gym bag so the guys wouldn't see it, but I always had it.

I went to my car, opened the trunk, opened the gym bag and looked at the bear. It still looked like new. I'd always kept it in a zip lock bag and I'd put it in a new bag, every year on her birthday... I opened the bag and took out the bear. It was brown and soft and had big button eyes.

I gave it one last squeeze and held it out for Chris.

"Here. I'd like her to have it."

America Inc.

Today, I am proud to announce my candidacy for President of the United States.

Whenever a man runs for the office of President, the first question you should ask him is "why?" Why do I feel the need to run, and why am I qualified for the most difficult job in the world?

Why do I feel the need to run? The answer is simple and clear: this country is in trouble and needs strong, decisive—proven leadership. For too long, the President has been a popularity contest, or a political tool, rather than a person with a proven track-record in managing millions of people and trillions of dollars.

To answer the second question—I have that track record, as CEO of GeneraEnergy, the world's single largest employer, and, I might add, most-profitable corporation. In this position I have successfully managed millions of men and women across the globe. All races, religions and beliefs. I have guided them towards clear goals. We have worked together, as a team, to ensure that the world's ever-growing need for energy has been met both affordably, and profitably.

Before I assumed this office, GeneraEnergy was in disarray, losing millions of jobs and billions of dollars, on the verge of bankruptcy. The board was talking of selling off the company as 49 separate groups, much as some today talk about removing the "United" from the "United" States.

I accepted this challenge when no one else would—because I was willing to put my money where my mouth is. To risk everything for the goal of bringing this once great corporation back to life, to improve the lives of its employees and customers.

And within four years—yes, the same as a Presidential term, I did just that. GeneraEnergy added 33% more new jobs, we went from losses to profits, and at the same time, we introduced new technology that was revolutionary.

That's what I am offering to do for you, as President of the United States.

First, to put my money where my mouth is—As the third richest man in the world, I will single handedly pay off the 2 trillion dollar national debt through a leveraged buyout. This means that on January 22nd, the country will immediately be free of the crushing debt that is undermining our recovery.

That means I am personally paying over $6,500 in debt that each of you hold to the US Government.

But that's just the start. In exchange for this debt payment, all I require is the ratification of a 28th amendment, which specifies my ability to run this country as a Capitalist Democratic Corporation, "America Inc."

Before there's any confusion, it's important to note that corporations, at their core, are democratic entities. Stockholders vote on board members and the president, just like American citizens do. So, importantly, it is still a government by the people and for the people.

The only difference is that in the corporation, it is not "one person, one vote," it is "one share, one vote." And, to start, every American receives one share in America Inc.

Naturally, these shares have value, and naturally they may be traded, openly and publicly. A citizen might, then, decide to sell their share to, say, their local Chevy dealer, and where they couldn't afford a car before, they can now. This instantly benefits our manufacturing and retail base.

Or, a mother or father might decide that their child's education is more important to their future than just one share, so they could sell or trade that share to an institution of higher learning to help secure their child's future. When that child turns 18, they receive a share, which they can do with what they please—giving them not just the power of a vote, but real financial power, as well.

Like other corporate shares, when American Inc. is profitable, yearly dividends are paid to shareholder citizens. Imagine that—your government pays you for our shared success!

I am promising each and every American a land where you have a real stake in the future. Where you can keep that stake and your vote, or trade it for opportunities for growth, entrepreneurship, and financial security.

You can, of course, see how this immediately changes the financial outlook of every citizen in the country—giving them new purchasing power. You can also see how it, then, behooves every American to work to keep the value of America Inc. shares high, as the value of the dollar is pegged directly to the value of shares.

In the New Office of the President, I will make the kind of sweeping changes so necessary to the failed enterprise that is this country. I will turn it around in a few short years, the way I did with GeneraEnergy.

Another solution I will implement within my first 100 days is single-payer national healthcare, which will be part of the nationalization of all hospitals and pharmaceutical companies. I know there are those out there who are afraid of larger government and more control, but these are people who don't understand the economies of scale.

As president of GeneraEnergy, I purchased HumanHealth, the country's third largest health insurance company, PharmCentra, the world's leading provider of generic pharmaceuticals, and Sustaina, then the country's third largest chain of hospitals, now the first.

In integrating this health network into GeneraEnergy, I was able to lower costs by upwards of 50%, while providing higher-quality healthcare, with fewer restrictions, to our 33 million employees, their families and partners. It was good for our people, and good for business.

GeneraHealth, a wholly owned subsidiary of GeneraEnergy, is ripe for a takeover by America

Inc., ready to provide that level of savings and improved coverage for all Americans.

When I took the reins of Genera, I worked tirelessly to cut waste from our system. I saw no need for 49 separate companies when 4 were more efficient.

In that same vein, I will order an immediate evaluation of every state in the corporation. Do we really need separate states of North and South Dakota, and Wyoming when their combined population is less than the city of Chicago? Likewise, North and South Carolina. Yes, the original 13 colonies have significant history, but do they deliver profitability to the nation's citizen shareholders?

Delaware, Rhode Island, New Hampshire, Maine—together they have a population less than Atlanta, Georgia. There are 14 states which, if combined, would still have fewer citizens than Los Angeles. In California, a senator represents 15 million people. In Wyoming it's just 300,000. That's not equitable. Clearly the state system is broken and needs to be revised.

The map of America Inc. includes just five states: New East, an area encompassing the eastern seaboard; New South: ranging from Texas to Florida; New MidWest: which integrates the heartland; New SouthWest: from the former New Mexico to what used to be Montana, and finally, New West: California, Nevada, Oregon, and Washington.

These five, new, powerful, vertically integrated company/states would each have a GNP to rival or beat the top 12 largest countries in the world. The New West, alone, would have an economy ranked #3 in the world, just behind America Inc, and China.

Instead of 50 different wasteful state governments, there are now only five. Our nation is 10 times more efficient overnight— streamlining government.

The increased efficiency of this more tightly integrated concentration of company/states would ensure that the United States remains United, at the time when some of the larger states, such as Texas and California, are becoming serious about secession. We cannot allow that to happen. Almost 300 years after our founding fathers united this country, I will not stand by and watch its dissolution.

As the great Abraham Lincoln said at the precipice of the Civil War, "I can not, and shall not, allow this great country to be torn apart for the wishes of the few, when we could be held together by the dreams of so many."

And that sums it up, my fellow Americans. We all have dreams—we are united by them. No matter who you are, where you come from, what you look like, where you pray, who you love—we all want the same things for our families—a good job, safe home, a healthy, happy family.

Those are all things I have provided to the 33 million employees of GeneraEnergy and its subsidiaries. And, through 10 times greater economies of scale, I can provide them to each and every shareholder in America Inc.

Together we can make this NEW American Dream more than a dream, we can make it a reality for ourselves and our children.

Realizing this dream for all requires the ability to not just accept, but embrace change, knowing that this change will lead to better days.

There will be those naysayers, stuck in the past, afraid of the future. But as in the past, Americans have not been afraid of change, we have welcomed it.

Thank you, and I look forward to having you work for me in this great new future.

Single Serving for Two

We met at the grocery store in the frozen food aisle. We were both leaning into the freezers for our single serving Lean Cuisine frozen dinners.

But in that moment, seeing us next to each other, reaching in at the same time, I said, "Is this sad? Buying these single servings?"

He said, "At least they taste good."

I agreed, "But it's better to share a meal with somebody. I haven't had dinner tonight have you?"

He said, "No."

I laughed, "You want to microwave these together?"

He laughed, "Why don't we go out to dinner?"

It's so weird because if there had been traffic, or if I'd decided to get cabbage before the frozen food... or if a million things had happened differently we never would have been standing there side by side in the frozen food case. We never would have met.

And sometimes it makes me overwhelmingly sad to think about all the people who are in traffic and miss their person standing there...

But the good news is that whenever brought us together in this strange, complicated world, we liked each other right from the start. It was always easy. I liked his shirt, shoes. I don't remember the pants he was wearing but I remember the shirt, it was one

of those really brightly colored plaid shirts—
so bright. And I was wearing a kitschy
Hawaiian shirt, with Tiki heads and Mai Tais.
Fun, but not so bright.

I'm sorry, I still cry when I think about this. I
still cry and try to decide "would it be better
if we'd never met and I never felt this
complete connection to another man?"
Because then I wouldn't have to feel... this
complete... ripping apart of my soul.

Oh, God. This feeling will pass. I'll think
about the good times. I'll think about the first
time he tried on my tiki shirt and I tried on
his bright plaid shirt and we saw each other.

I will remember how soft his beard was, and
how slightly rough his fingers were. I will
remember looking into his gray green eyes
and wondering what this creature was and
how'd I gotten lucky enough to meet him.

And I knew he felt the same about me,
because he told me. At last I had met
someone who gave me as much as I gave
him.

I mostly remember not thinking at all when I was laying with his arms around me and his furry chest tickling my nose. I loved that. It reminded me of the childhood teddy bear I squeezed so tight it changed its shape.

And that's how I felt about Dwight—he changed my shape with his hugs. He made me stand straighter and walk with my head held high.

Oh, God. I'm glad that I met him even if I had to lose him. Even if I had to watch him die slowly from cancer. At least I could be the person who was there for him. At least I could still be looking in his eyes.

As he got thinner and weaker, I was the one to put my arms around him. To feel him bury his face against my chest. He would get so angry with himself and apologize for being sick.

I would always say, "You have nothing to apologize for. If I could have made it me instead of you I would."

But I don't know who it was harder for. He's moved on to another world—to another life—

somewhere hopefully I will be with him again.

And I am here. With just the smell of his shirts, my happy memories, and my single serving frozen dinner.

Fountain of Love

"**A**rrivaderci," I sighed, throwing my new wedding ring into the Trevi fountain, then instantly regretting it as I could have taken it to a pawn shop. So off went my new Gucci loafers and into the fountain I strode, followed with surprising speed by a policewoman wearing a one-piece swimsuit in blue with gold piping.

"ARRESTARE!" she yelled, and I pretended I didn't speak Italian.

But she was not to be deterred and moved with such alarming swiftness that I wondered if she was from a special order of mermaid officers.

Still, I reached down and pulled out what I thought was my wedding ring, but was actually a napkin ring from the adjacent Cafe Trevi. I threw it back towards the cafe as an act of good Karma and kept reaching.

"ARRESTO!" she shrieked again in the way that mermaids might have done to deafen sailors.

"NO COMPRENDE!" I yelled back, still sifting through the coins at the bottom.

"STOP IT, ASSHOLE," She cried, unavoidably understandable.

"Oh, I'm sorry, I dropped my wedding ring..." I said back at a normal tone which was then difficult to hear over the rushing of waters.

"I saw you throw it."

"I was angry."

"You were stupid, now get out."

"I was grief-stricken."

"You're an idiot."

"I saw my wife kissing our tour guide, Guido."

"Guido? Angelucci?"

"Yes. Big hairy ugly brute of a man."

"He's my husband!"

"Handsome brute of a man?"

"He kisses everyone"

"He didn't kiss me."

"Ladies, you fool."

"I'm a fool but I'm no lady."

With that she reached down and raised her wet hand triumphantly holding my ring.

"I am going to keep this," she said, laughing.

"May it remind you that your husband is an adulterer!" I started to cry, genuine tears, seemingly indistinguishable from the fountain spray hitting my face.

"We will go back to your hotel and fuck, then you will feel better."

This officer, this woman, was clearly a mermaid, trying to entrap me to my doom. I immediately accepted.

"Hotel Arbietti, room 601." I said.

She took my hand and led me to steps I didn't even know existed so it was easy to exit the surprisingly frigid waters. It was only now that I felt the cold.

There was another officer waiting with warmed Turkish towels.

"Leonardo, I'm going to go fuck this gentleman," she said.

"Of course, Grizelda, I'll keep watch."

My loafers were gone, of course, stolen by a ragamuffin, hooligan or resale shop owner. No mind, the cobblestones were warm and smooth on my feet.

"Do you fuck everyone who jumps in the fountain?" I asked, tentatively, yet not really caring about the answer.

"I am not a whore. Only the handsome English ones who cry. I find that very sexy."

We were holding hands. Wrapped in towels. Nobody seemed to notice much less care. The blue had returned to the sky. The colors of the buildings were more intense, pink, violet, azure, teal, red.

"Why do you stay with him?" I asked, again, wondering why I couldn't just leave well enough alone and get on with it.

"Ha! He is a fantastic fuck. You will be lucky to be as good. I will tell you if you are, or are not."

I had my answer, which now felt more like a challenge, but I was up for it. I was angry, and nothing made me randier than fury.

As we entered the hotel I wondered what I would do if my wife was in the room? What would I do if she wasn't in the room? Well, I'd be very sad, then I'd have sex with a mermaid, that's what I'd do, as we padded across the lobby's surprisingly soft carpet and the elevator operator averted his eyes.

"Sesto piano" the mermaid said in Italian. The elevator cage rattled up and I looked down at the growing protuberance under my towel. The mermaid noticed, too, and rubbed herself up against me.

The elevator door opened and she got out first, pulling me down the hall.

"I must hurry, I only have an hour for lunch," she said, which made me wonder what she ate for lunch? Perhaps fish, from the fountain. Perhaps me? I didn't care.

I fished around in my pants pocket to find the key and opened the door. I went in first to see if Claudia... no, she wasn't here. The mermaid charged past me.

"OK, sailor, fuck me!" she cried, tearing off her towel and stripping off her suit.

She was stunning! Breathtaking! Maybe the most beautiful creature I had ever seen on two legs. In fact, I was momentarily surprised and relieved by the fact that she had two legs, both equally shapely and sensuous instead of a mermaid tail.

Off went my towel. Shirt. Pants. And underwear that kept sticking to me as I tirelessly tore at it.

I, too, leaped on the bed, throwing caution to the wind and allowing my skin to touch the bedspread which every guidebook on the planet had warned against.

The room became a blur of color and sound and chlorine scented skin. Lips and nipples and arguably the most beautiful buttocks since Venus. We did unspeakable things to each other which I wanted so desperately to speak about but she kept holding her hand to my mouth. It felt both demeaning, as if she was silencing me, and thrilling, as if she was silencing me.

Was there nothing this creature would not do? Would it end with her drowning or devouring me? I no longer cared. I had lost all civilized thought in a frenzy of pure animal lust.

Our congress reached its fevered peak of moans and squeaks (that would have been me), and supernova-like explosions (also me) just when I heard the door open.

And there was Claudia, in her pink sweater set, mouth agape.

At first I thought perhaps there might be some excuse I could make, but, fuck it, it was what it was, and what it was was so ethereal, magical, carnal, surprising and glorious I didn't care who saw.

Was Claudia shocked? Angry? Sad? I couldn't tell as she stood there, frozen.

I looked from Claudia to the mermaid back to Claudia, who dropped her shopping bag in shock, then quickly picked it up and turned to go.

"GUIDO?" the mermaid's shriek returned.

Claudia froze and looked around uneasily.

"So che ci sei, cornea pezzo di merda stronzo."

Claudia's fingers began to wiggle, oddly, and she turned and tried to shut the door. But just then, a large hand reached around and opened it. Guido. In the flesh, or at least what little could be seen of it under all that hair.

"HA HA HA HA HA!" the mermaid shrieked so loud and so close I wondered if I would permanently lose my hearing. I didn't care. I'd never been so satisfied. I felt myself sliding out of her and I lay back on the filthy bedspread, naked and unashamed.

"È una scopata migliore di te" she whispered now, like a warm sirocco wind. "He is a better fuck then you, Guido," she said in English, for which I'll ever be grateful, because otherwise I wouldn't have known what the she said, and neither would Claudia.

"Questo è impossibile con il suo pene circonciso" he grunted, sounding more hurt than angry.

"He said 'that's impossible with his circumcised pecker'" she said, shaking her head while kindly translating. "Il suo cazzo è molto più dolce del tuo" she continued, without translation.

Claudia still hadn't moved. It was as if she was surprised I'd caught her in a compromising position, not that she'd caught me in one. And I simply no longer cared. The mermaid and I would sail off into the sunset together, forever making beautiful love by and in the Mediterranean. I had never been happier.

Then Guido pushed past a still frozen Claudia and sat on the bed next to us, which I found uncomfortable if not outright rude, not to mention more than a little frightening given the size of his massive paws.

"Ma io sono l'uomo che ti ama. Ti amo con tutto il mio cuore, anima e pene."

The mermaid went "Eh." Then she whispered to me, "He says he loves me with all his heart and soul and penis."

"That's actually quite sweet," I said, "And sad, because you are mine now."

She looked at me quizzically.

"What you say?"

"We shall be together now, my love!"

That's when she started laughing. Not pretty little giggling at all as she threw her head back and made grotesque croaking and gasping sounds like a vampire choking on the Pope. Then Guido joined her, sounding like a hyena having an epileptic seizure.

He leaned in and kissed her, a kiss that seemed to go on for as long as our entire love making session. It went on so long that finally Claudia and I locked eyes in confusion.

I rolled off the other side of the bed and wrapped myself in the towel.

Guido had removed his shirt, though it was not immediately obvious because he had been wearing brown wool and still looked like he was.

I walked by Claudia towards the bathroom, as casually as I could under the circumstances. I needed a shower from the combination of the fountain and the bedspread and the possible mermaid STDs.

But as I was closing the door, there was Claudia, following me. She closed the door, which is good because the noise coming from the bedroom was increasingly alarming and I found myself inexplicably engorged again.

Claudia looked at me in a way I absolutely didn't recognize. Was it anger? Disgust? Sadness? Confusion?

It didn't matter. We'd never done it in the shower before, and now I was a merman.

Same prayer, different gods

From the journal of Juan Carlos Almonte, dated 1579. Translated in 1922 by Steven Carlisle, New York Central Library. Original journal lost during WWII.

17. June, in the year of our Lord 1579.

Antonio Sevilla, our cook, passed today. The 13th member of the crew to leave this ship, this earth, this life. They have suffered, yet they have been spared the suffering the rest of us wake to every morning. Morning after morning of nothing but sea, for four long months. Victuals low. Tempers high.

I tended to Antonio, as I did to the rest. They call me "Doc" and beg me to help, but I have been unable to help any of them. They look into my eyes with the terror of death and beg me to save them. I say to pray to God, because only he can save us. Only he can. But he does not.

I do not know why.

He is a vengeful God, my God, their God—so much the same, but the difference nearly killed me. I had to flee my shop, my city, my love, because my God is different. Yet my God is as vengeful and uncaring as theirs— why? I do not understand how a father can treat his children this way. If I had children I would give them nothing but love.

But my love has limited power, as I have learned.

Jorge DeSilva was the first to leave us, but he earned his exit. He discovered my secret, perhaps when I was washing, I do not know. He is the one to start calling me "Doc" in a mocking way. I thought at first it was because I was a butcher back home—so at least I knew anatomy—if only of animals.

But Jorge was an animal, cruel, dangerous. Everyone was afraid of him. The other men were too ignorant to know the Venetian custom of calling Jews "Doc." It didn't matter that we might save their life, they still despised us, locked us in our ghettos at night until they needed us.

I could not risk the crew knowing. So while I was in the larder, I found a bad piece of meat. Oh, God, please forgive me, or kill me soon, the guilt is too much to bear. I hid the bad part of the meat inside and Antonio, our cook, prepared it special for Jorge.

Jorge became sick, that was my hand, but his dying was God's will. And my hand was only a servant of God's will, no?

Jorge was the first to look in my eyes and beg me to save him. But I could not. Would not.

Together we prayed—but different prayers. Mine was answered. That was the only time.

As three men hoisted Jorge overboard, it was I who led the prayer for God to have mercy upon his soul. This time I hoped it would not be answered, but perhaps that hope doomed my future prayers.

As he fell into the sea, I crossed myself—crossed myself in the sight of all the men—and my God. It was my protection, just as it was theirs. Only as I did it, I felt betrayal and fear. For myself, for all of us. He was the only man I ever hurt and only because he was hurting others.

But, as happens during long voyages, other men, good men, kind men with families back home, they became sick, delirious, weak, vomitous, cold humours. I could do nothing for them but be there, and pray with them. Pray—the same prayer but to different Gods.

One by one they fell. Now 13, the number of the devil. I was not the only one counting, the rest of the men were sore afraid. Even the great captain Drake, who must always seem strong lest the weak mutiny and turn back, knows he is just a man, on God's great sea.

I remember the first time I saw Drake, with his ridiculous English hat. It was the worst day of my life.

All I wanted is what other men had—a wife and children, a family. My mother had died in childbirth and my father went to Africa to find his fortune, so I became "the ugly one" as my aunt called me. As her children called me.

And it was true, I was ugly—I am ugly. Short. Wide. With a pushed-in face like a muff dog. The first time I saw one of these dogs in the sleeve of a rich woman, I thought perhaps I would have the same luck—a woman, any woman, might want me for warmth at least. But no, it was not to be.

I apprenticed as a butcher in Valencia because it was a trade where I would always eat, this is what my Aunt Azalia told me, as she pushed me out of the house and I lived in the filthy back room of Senior Bastita's butcher shop.

But I was good at this—strong and skilled with the knife, seeing the beauty of the work, learning the art of butchery. And Senior Bastita's customers noticed the difference of meat that was prepared with care—cut correctly rather than most cheaply. So while at first he scolded me for preparing meat that cost him more—as his business grew he did not care, he just worked me harder.

I was at the age of finding a wife, and I hoped my profession and access to food would make me more attractive in the eyes of potential father-in-laws. But most were afraid of me, the knives, the blood. Only the poorest considered me.

Pedro Manquisto was such a man. With three daughters he was desperate to find a wife for Margarita. Desperate enough to consider me.

"I am a good man," I told him and I could see in his eyes he did not care. His daughter, Rosa, was a tiny little thing. She looked frightened when she first laid eyes upon me. She asked to be left alone with her papa. I complied, but still heard her call me a "cow." Her father said, "A bull, he is big and strong." But I knew.

As the wedding plans progressed, I thought perhaps this is how all women were. Fearful of the male's strength. And when I would walk with Rosa, her mother two steps behind us always, I believed she saw me in a new way. I was allowed to hold her hand, so tiny, like a capon, and she would tell me "You are so warm, Rojo," she called me "The Bull" in a way I thought to be affectionate.

The wedding neared. I put aside the best meat for the festival. Then, two days before, her mother found Rosa in her room, hanging from a rope.

At first her father said it must be Andreas, a neighbor boy. He had loved her and killed her in anger. But I knew. Why must I always know? Andreas had been hunting with his father, and soon the whispers were that she had been possessed... or with child, my demonic child, and the shame was too much.

But she was not with child from holding my hand. Or possessed. Or weak of mind. I knew. Why must I always know? Why must I be able to hear the whispers?

After this Senior Bastita's business slowed— he, too, put the blame on me. Then Rosa's papa came to me with her dowry. He said that Father Augusto had told him he must make good on his promise or Rosa would not go to heaven. I told him I would not take it. He begged me, for her soul.

I accepted, knowing what it meant, that half must go to Father Augusto. It was a dirty business in a dirty place, and I used the rest of the money to move to Barcelona. Start a new life, open my own shop.

I did well there. People were sophisticated and appreciated my work, my artistry. As a shop owner I was more attractive to the fathers of young women.

Senior DaCosta brought his daughter to see me. They saw nothing wrong with me. His daughter, who I will not name in the sight of God for what I will tell, was a girl of considerable size, which I liked. I did not feel monstrous with her. She was also bawdy and we laughed and spent time alone together, knowing each other in the Biblical way. This was love. This was the start of the life I had always wanted.

Yet this was the end, too. Someone from Valencia, I suspect it was Father Augusto, was spreading words of my birth—that I was a Jew. I received a letter from her father, saying I had deceived him of my status and the marriage offer was void. I knew his daughter must have known and did not care —but I did not see her again.

Then word spread, which was dangerous with the Church persecuting my kind. When I found a Star of David painted on my door in blood, my store ransacked and my meat stolen, I did not return.

I took what I had, gold sewn into my coat lining, and the beef I had been drying into Cecina, and I headed for the docks. I would find a ship and sail away. It was all I could think of.

That is when I met Captain Drake, with his ridiculous hat and his bottle green coat that was too warm for this time of year. But it made him look rich, and powerful, and that was the point. He wanted all to see that he was not like the other captains who offered you gold when you stepped upon the ship only to take it from you when you were dead. I had heard the stories.

Captain Drake offered you gold when you reached the New World, a place where streets were paved with it, he said.

He, too, was called "The Butcher," in his case for his slaughter of the Spanish Armada, and he was here for supplies and men—which he expected to be given to him.

He would not take just anyone—a man had to bring strength and skill—or, in my case, 50 pounds of Cecina, and the strength of a bull—a word he used, too, now in a good way.

I recall stepping on the ship—I had never been on one before, and it wouldn't stop moving. Much to the enjoyment of the other men I was sick several times that day, and watched as my old life, my shop, my love, grew smaller in the distance. Never to be seen again.

When I joined the crew I had heard sailor's stories about illness and mermaids calling men to their death. I knew that half of us would be dead by the time we found land. Maybe I would be one of the lucky ones and die. I had lost everything, so I would lose my life, too.

But I did not become sick like the other men. And Jorge named me "Doc" and the rest of the men treated me with respect. Captain Drake, became less aloof, he shared his spirits with me, told me stories of England which sounded as treacherous as anything I had encountered. I told him of my life, and he said it was best behind me.

"The sea washes away our past," he said, with a tear in his eye—he had lost not just something, but someone, too.

Every night I pray to God that I will either live, or die. That the choice is his. And even today, when I awoke before dawn, in the dark, I knew the choice was his.

Every day I think I have spotted land, in the distance. I have hope that we will land, the sea having washed away my past. I will kiss mother earth, never again to step on a boat.

Every day, as the sun rises in the sky, what I think is land is a piece of driftwood, or a cloud bank looking like a cliff.

Our supplies run low. Our hope runs low. We survive on the fish we catch and the dew we capture on the sails. The fish are small, the water bitter. And the mysteries, endless. We once saw a fish bigger than our ship— spouting steam from the top of its black head. The men thought we could eat forever on that fish, and I thought it could eat us all. Neither happened as it disappeared into the deep.

Do I see a cliff? Or a cloud? I will know with the sunrise.

I pray it is a cliff. Perhaps God will answer this last prayer.

Any God.

Children of the Moon

I t had been too many years since my last ballet. It was poorly received, critics calling it "old-fashioned" and worse, "dull."

I felt I had let down my company of dancers, so I became more of a figurehead. The company, after all, bore my name, *The Oligo Project*. I allowed my young protege, Brette Webber, to take the lead as creative director.

Under her direction, the company produced a series of modern dances utilizing video, web, and other technologies that charmed the critics and made me cringe.

That was not dance. That was social media with feet. I felt more sorry for my dancers now than when they were dancing beautifully for critics who did not care, or more accurately, understand.

During one of these "performances," the audience could "tweet" suggestions to the dancers. They were then expected to improvise on such thrilling topics as "grapefruit," and "puppies," and most mortifying, yet delightful to the inebriated audience, "sodomy." Truly disgusting.

I watched the dancers who had spent their lives training, literally working themselves to the bone, having to perform lurid acts onstage, and decided it was time to remove my name from the company.

I took a taxi home, sobbing in the back seat, tears for myself, for my dancers, for the future of dance.

After Jacques died, I lived alone, which was fine, except in times like this when I so desperately needed a shoulder to cry on and an ear to whisper into.

I called my former prima ballerina, Jesse St. Louis, known for her rough yet deeply emotional interpretations and begged her to come over.

She ran a catering business now. They were, at this moment, catering the after party for the big money patrons of the dance company. She promised to come as soon as they had packed up.

In the meantime, I got rip-roaringly plastered while looking through years of scrapbooks from the company. There was Jesse, thrilling in *Clair De Lune*, where she held the stage by herself while the rest of the company danced in the aisles. I always thought the Broadway show CATS stole this idea from me. But what was one to do except look at it as an "homage" and take it as a compliment?

And there were photos of Jacques, as I first met him. Only 19 years old—yet with the oldest soul I'd ever encountered. Fresh off the boat from Cuba where, disguised as a waiter on a cruise ship, he had managed to escape from a land where there was little possibility for him to perform.

I remember his audition for me like it was yesterday—his posture, his presence, his passion. We all sat in awe as he seemed to fly across the room barely touching the floor. When he stopped, I was too much in shock—and love—to know what to do. He looked as if we did not like his dancing, but I gave him a standing ovation, shouted, "Bravo!" and welcomed him to the company, and my life.

I was 15 years older and had reached the age where I was no longer able to dance the way I once had, so it was a joy to dance vicariously through him. And he needed someone to tell him what to do—a dancer without choreography is lost (at least before the invention of twitter).

And so, with his fiery stage presence, and my cerebral and conceptual choreography, we lit the world of dance like Nijinsky and Diaghilev.

We traveled the world, performing for royalty and sold out houses. We loved the dance, and each other.

But too soon, Jacques, too, was too old to do what he once did. He danced well into his 40's, but he no longer flew.

Audiences dwindled. Times and tastes changed. And the once-shocking dances I had created, like "quadruped" where the dancers performed with shoes both on their hands and their feet, were now considered passé.

Then Jacques contracted Lyme disease at our Connecticut home and the pain in his joints made it impossible to dance. He felt he had nothing left to give.

I insisted to everyone who would listen that it was an accident when he was hit and killed by a taxi, but in my heart, I knew it might not be.

And then I was alone—with a failing company. So, fine, let the next generation come to the fore...

The last photo I have with Jacques was at the first show choreographed by Brette. It was early in her tenure so dance still mattered to her more than marketing.

Her piece was a lovely tribute to Jacques, taking his most famous solos and distributing them to every dancer in the company, including the women. She arranged them into his life story, from escaping Cuba to his last days on stage.

Jacques and I were both devastated by this— it was gorgeous but so sad.

And now, if I give up the company, what will I have? The occasional tribute from other dance troupes performing my old works, so often "re-visualized" by their creative directors into something I would find unrecognizable. I would sit in the audience, enduring the dance with a fake smile on my face, and say nice things to everyone afterwards, then go back to the hotel and drink myself into oblivion.

My time was up.

Just as I headed towards the bathroom, wondering if I had enough Valium to sleep forever, Jesse arrived, bearing beefsteak and cheesecake, my favorites. They were left over from the party—more accurately, she had set them aside for me. What a darling girl she was.

I proceeded to cry and moan and whine and otherwise make a damned fool of myself for almost an hour, during which time she fed me, did the dishes, sat on the sofa and cradled me in her arms.

"You are not over yet, my brilliant friend," she told me, with a voice so sincere I almost believed her. And how difficult must it have been for her to say that when her time was over.

"But don't you miss it?" I couldn't stop myself from asking her.

"Miss the dance?" she sputtered, starting to laugh. "Miss the endless work, the constant pain, the throwing up, the overwhelming stage fright that never went away, the terror before the show and depression after it? Do I miss that? No, Henry, I do not miss that, thank you."

"Then do you blame me for putting you through that?" I asked, now wondering how many lives I had ruined.

"You're being an idiot," she said, lovingly. "Dance was all I ever wanted to do and I'm glad I did it. Now I get to eat steak and cheesecake and I don't care how fat I am."

She wasn't fat, but she wasn't bone thin the way ballerinas are expected to be.

"Choreographers can still work out of wheelchairs, you don't have to stop," she told me, sternly.

"Nobody cares what I do," I lamented.

"Pity, party of one," she rolled her eyes. "Fine, I always have room for you at one of my steam tables. Does that make you feel better?"

She always knew just what to say.

"Now that I've been a complete narcissistic ass..."

"As usual," she interrupted.

"As usual," I repeated, "What can I do for you my love?"

"Create a new dance for me. And your other retired dancers. Something we can do that's full of emotion without being full of jumps. Let us actually enjoy the dance instead of it being a terrifying ordeal."

She looked at me with those eyes that looked like a Siamese cat's. Blue with flecks of gold and that heavy black eyeliner. I always thought she was the most beautiful woman in the world, and I still did.

"Anything for you, my pet," I told her as she took my hand and led me to my bed and tucked me in.

"Be right back," she murmured as she left. I heard her in the bathroom, the toilet flushing.

Then she crawled in bed with me and cuddled up, completely naked. Our bodies felt again as they once did, warm, sensual, skin against skin.

She whispered in my ear, "I flushed the Valium down the toilet, my love, now let's go to sleep."

And I did—better than I had slept since Jacques died.

In the morning Jesse called me from the kitchen. She had made biscuits and bacon and eggs and everything was ready, except for me.

"Out of bed, sleepy head!" she called. I pulled on my caftan and shuffled into the kitchen.

"I never eat breakfast," I said, kissing her on the cheek.

"It's after 1, this is brunch."

"Oh, in that case," I said, sitting at the table.

I couldn't remember the last time anything tasted this good.

"Thank you, my dear, for staying with me, for this, for your beauty and talent and love."

"P-shaw," she said, slapping my hand for the last piece of bacon.

"Oh, oh!" I said, surprised. She looked alarmed, as if I was having a stroke.

"I just remembered something! A dream from last night!"

She seemed more interested in the artisanal cherry jam than my revelation.

"It's the gift you wanted. I dreamt the ballet," I told her, and she stopped chewing.

"Tell me!" she growled, adorably, like Tammy Grimes.

"But first, some music," I said, finding my phone and searching for just the right piece.

"Of course I'll have to commission a new score for this, but what I heard in my dream was something like this..." I said as I started to play Bernstein conducting "Cavalluccio."

"The seahorse!" Jesse was literally on the edge of her seat—her feet en pointe.

"It's called 'Children of the Moon,'" I told her, setting the scene.

"The stage is black, then specs of light appear, first on the cyc, like stars, then spreading to the floor. We see a dancer onstage, but we can only see her through these spots of light.

"She—you—are wearing white, with sleeves that trail down to your toes. You are wearing slippers, not toe shoes, none of that.

"You are curled in a fetal position, and another dancer I call 'mother' stands in front of you. Suddenly—a sharp spotlight from below casts a shadow on the cyc—so it looks like the mother is giving birth to you—then she leaps from the spotlight—and the light becomes the moon."

Jesse's eyes widened.

"You are born under the August sky, so you are named Augusta. We can use that projector Brette bought for the twitter shit to project your name as if it's floating out of your mouth as you dance, like a child.

"Then, as the moon rises, so do you—you are literally dancing on air, floating."

"Ooh, that sounds easy on the joints!" she said.

"Don't interrupt an artiste at work!" I said. She giggled.

"As you float, we hit you with a pinpoint spot, so you appear to be the brightest star in the sky. The stars in the background move down, making you appear to be going up, but you're really landing back on the stage—the surface on the moon!"

"Oooh," she couldn't help but say.

"The moon is a turntable, half black, half white, like the sides of the moon. You, in white, are on the dark side of the moon."

"I love symbolism!" she sighed.

"You've been warned, my love," I admonished her playfully. "You do a dance to mother moon—I see something like what I had you do in "Velostrotude," only as if weightless..."

"That'll be a trick," she sniggered.

"Do you want me to give your part to someone else, maybe Cleo?"

"You wouldn't dare. Fine, I'll stop interrupting, so go, my calves are twitching!"

"You will actually be weightless, my love, because you will still be attached to the flying harness—so your feet will never touch the ground. Yes, I have thought of everything. Then as the turntable moves clockwise, you recede to the darkness in the back and we see someone new."

"Who? Sorry, but who?" she asked.

"Antonio, Fabrizio, Bobby, you choose."

"I choose you!" she said, through toast crumbs.

"Stop it, I'm far too old for this," I shook my head.

"Not if you're weightless you're not. Isn't that the point of all this? It could be your tribute to Jacques."

Now she had me—I stared at her.

"Fine, it's me. I'm dressed in black on the light side of the moon. My name is Augustus. I dance virtually the same solo you did—but in a completely masculine way."

"I LOVE it!" she cried, "I totally, absolutely love it, it's divine!"

"It's not over."

"I know, I know, but I see where you're going..."

"If you know so much tell me what happens next. Tell me how predictable I've become..."

"Not at all, love, what I imagine happening is that I'm dancing and my side and you on yours and poignantly, we never meet."

"Wrong!" I cry with delight. "Just exactly the opposite! At the moment when light becomes dark—we see each other, across the crepuscule."

"The what?"

"The twilight, the dusk, my light fades into you."

"Yes, of course, I can see it!"

"As the light becomes dark, our bodies merge, our fingers touch, like the Sistine chapel, then our hands join in a suspended pas de deux that slowly, weightlessly takes us from two forms into one, single, spinning whole!"

"As this happens, the spotlight on us creates a lunar eclipse in the background—the stars grow brighter and spread off the lip of the stage, into the audience, so they, too, are filled with stars!

With that I collapsed onto the sofa—I hadn't even realized I was doing the dance myself as I spoke.

Jesse had tears streaming down her face.

"Oh, my love! You have told the life story of not just a human being, but an artist! Being born, finding ourselves, escaping the gravity of expectations, doing our own unique dances, integrating with our shadow-self and finally becoming one with the cosmos. It's gorgeous."

"I saw it as clearly as if I was watching from the wings," I told her.

"I saw it, too. So beautiful. So moving. We must do it, Henry, we must, we must, we must!"

Oh what the hell.

I called Brette and asked her if she had room for something old-fashioned, or even just plain old.

She said it would make for a wonderful fundraiser, and perhaps a PBS special and it was just the kind of historic brand building... something... I so rarely understood what she said except for the word 'yes!'"

Every joint and muscle ached. The flying harnesses hurt like hell. It was heaven.

Tomorrow didn't come

I was never good with women. Not even with my wifes.

I never know what they wanted. But I wanted them.

I thought if I was bigger I could have given them what they wanted, a big strong man. So I was strong, but I was not big.

When I grew up in Nagasaki, I never saw any foreigners. Most people were about the same. But I was smaller than the other boys. And they made fun of me, called me "Little sister" like I was a girl.

One day Akio called me this and I got so mad I wanted to hit him, and I tried. My arms were flying but I didn't hit anything and then because he was bigger he just grabbed me and held my arms and I couldn't do anything. He didn't hurt me, except my pride, and after that the boys called me 乳飲み子 which means "suckling child" which is worse.

I was the size of a girl, and I played with them and they would dress me up. I liked them but I knew we were different and when they would dress me they would make fun of my chinchin because it was sticking out.

My father was a merchant. He sold supplies for the ships that would come into the harbor. Big rope, bigger than my body, and pulleys and also tar and shipbuilding things. Everything was so heavy.

I wanted to help, but my father said I was too small. I could only help by sweeping and keeping clean, like a girl. My mother taught me how to cook in case that was the only job I could get.

When I was 12, I got a little bigger, still small, but not as small. I told my father I would help him carry things to the barges. He said I was still too small. I said I was not and I would prove it, and I did.

There was a big pulley, made of metal, and it weighed more than I did, but I used all my effort to drag it outside. And then there was the barge, sitting high in the canal. How could I get it up there? I piled up boxes and one at a time rolled the pulley up the boxes into the barge. It took all afternoon but I did it, and that is when my father saw that I could do things like a boy.

That summer I worked for him, carrying things, getting stronger. Not taller, but at least strong. So when Haru made fun of me one day, I pulled him into an alley and I hit and hit and hit him until he was bloody and crying. I did not feel bad for this. Haru was mean and would often take things from little children.

After this, nobody made fun of me, and they all called me "Kenta" which means "strong."

That summer, father gave me money for my good work, and I saved it. I saved it for a girl. Rei. Her father ran the store across the street selling canned goods for the sailors. And I would think how lovely it must be to have a store full of food, so fancy in those silver cans. Beans and fruit all year round, and meat, too. Meat in silver cans. I never had that.

Rei and I would take tea together, and one day she brought a silver can of tuna. It was a beautiful thing. No bones or skin or head, just the perfect flesh. Like her. And we ate it together and I wanted to touch her.

I reached over for the can and my hand touched her hand and we looked at each other. I felt hot and she turned pink, like a flower blooming in the springtime. And I reached up to touch her pink cheek, it was so beautiful. She giggled and pulled away and I said I was sorry and she said I did not need to be sorry, and she took my hand and put it back on her cheek.

I did not know what was happening but I felt this, well, you know, and I leaned in and kissed her cheek, and it was soft and warm, like a baby, but better, like the winter air had frosted her with soft white hairs. And I noticed everything about her, the shape of her nose and her eyelashes and the way her hair grew out of her head.

Then I heard her father calling for her and she jumped up and I thought maybe I had done something wrong but she whispered "tomorrow" and left.

But tomorrow didn't come.

My father sent me out on the three-wheeled bicycle cart to the country to collect more rope from the rope makers who grew hemp and braided it into huge coils. I could carry two coils on my bicycle.

It took two hours to ride to where they made the rope on Kanawa Island. It was August and still hot but it was a beautiful day and I was happy to ride.

I had stopped for some Jukimi, a late summer squash soup and I threw rice to the water birds and watched the ripples in the river.

I rode my bike next to a ditch used to irrigate the rice fields. The wind rushed against my face as my leg kept a steady beat. The day felt musical.

And then, I don't remember this part very well but there was a sound so loud like the moon had fallen to the ground.

That's what I thought, the story of Komi and Yama, the gods of the land and sky and how they would kiss and make thunder.

I was in the ditch in the water but still feeling very hot, and the sky was dark and I didn't know what was happening.

I was almost 14 but I was afraid like the little girl they had called me.

Then thousands of little silver fish floated to the top of the water all around me, dead. Yet somehow the fish were comforting to me, like a blanket on the water, like Komi was holding me.

I crawled out of the water. It was hotter than I remembered and it smelled very bad, burnt and ashes.

It started to rain but not water, gray flakes like snow but bigger and dry and very soft— like Rei's cheek—but they turned to nothing when I touched them.

My bicycle tires were flat. I wondered why my head felt so hot and when I reached up to brush away my hair there was nothing there but my skin. I still do not have hair.

I was alone and thought maybe I must be dead and in jigoku, hell. But why? For touching Rei when we were not betrothed?

The sun never set—there was an orange light coming from the city.

I wanted to go home—but I was so tired. I lay there by the side of the ditch and I slept, all the way through the night. It was never cold.

In the morning I set off towards home.

I saw no other people. Surely I had been damned and was alone in the world.

Then I saw the worst thing I have ever seen—worse even than what I saw later, because this was the line between the living and the dead.

A real line. On one side there was green grass and an old brown yado house with an apple tree, standing as it always had, full of red apples.

On the other was only black and gray, no color.

Between them, this deadly white line, like the hand of God had written on the earth. It ran in a straight line for as far as my eyes could see. To the west. To the east.

I touched the line. It was warm. I walked over the line to the other side.

I didn't know where I was. There were no landmarks. No Kozan temple. No Bukan shrine. No marketplace tents. No street signs or street lamps or even buildings, just rubble.

There were no people, but there were strange noises, crackling sounds, like the earth was in pain.

I kept looking for home. I do not know why I thought it would be there when nothing else was, but I wanted to go there. Surely I had crossed over into hell, but at least my family would be there with me.

That's when I saw the giants. I had never seen people so tall, or pale or with strange eyes in odd colors—like the sky and sea. Were they monsters? They were white with no skin, their weird eyes behind portholes. I felt naked in my cotton yukata.

And small, I felt so small.

One of these giants yelled at me and now I was so scared. What would they do to me? And, as strong as I thought I was, I started to cry.

The giant came up to me and picked me up. He said, something I could not understand, but I could tell he was not angry, and he held me like I was being held by a kind bear.

I couldn't stop shaking.

He took me to a jeep and held onto me while we drove. And we stopped at tents and he took me inside and they waved things over me that made noises like snapping twigs and they looked at each other like something was bad.

One man washed me all over with a rough cloth and wrapped me in white cotton that was soft. I didn't understand what anyone was saying. And I could not stay awake.

The next morning I awoke crying. I wanted to go home, to be with my father and mother, for things to be like they were. Why hadn't I been home with them? We would be together if I had not gone to the countryside.

Finally I saw a Japanese man, the first I had seen, and he was wearing white, like me.

"Take me home, take me home," I begged him, crying.

"Your home is gone," he said

I screamed, "you are wrong!"

But he was right.

Yoshi. That was his name. Even after all these years I still remember it. He said our world had ended and I was going to live in a new world.

The way he said it made me think that this must happen sometimes and it was normal and I would be OK.

Then he held my hand as we walked up the stairs onto a big airplane. I remember thinking it was like a boat but the engine screws were in the air. And it made a loud noise and was shaking and I got scared again.

He held me close and later told me to look out the window.

My new world was heaven.

I was so hungry he could hear my stomach over the noise of the engines. He opened a can of tuna. I remembered Rei. And the day that never came.

The Unnecessary

"Do the unnecessary." Those were his words. Maharishi Varantu. On his deathbed. To me.

I was the only one who'd heard them. I'd only started volunteering at the hospital three days ago. I had been living on the street and was starving and cold and I knew the hospital was warm and had food. So I put on the plaid shirt and pants I kept clean and I said, "I want to help people," because I did, I wanted to help people, not just myself.

The big nurse, Mrs. Baker said, "Yes, of course, we can use a volunteer like you," so I started working. I delivered food, propped people up and saw if they needed anything. I kept them company. Most just didn't want to be alone, and I was happy I could be there for them.

I was told by Mrs. Baker that my job would be to provide comfort, and I liked that very much. I could provide comfort for others as well as myself. When I wasn't helping others, I found an empty room where I could help myself. A small store room full of sheets and blankets where I could squeeze into a shelf surrounded by warmth and softness and sleep.

I was just about to go to sleep there when the maharishi was brought in. He had stepped on a nail that went through his sandal. It happened several weeks ago and he told his followers he was fine, but he started to swell and develop a fever and found it hard to speak, so they brought him, wearing his beautiful orange robes.

I heard heavy footsteps coming close, so I jumped up and looked like I was collecting sheets.

"Oh, good, you're already on it, follow me," said Mrs. Baker.

I helped her make up the bed as he was wheeled in and made sure he was made comfortable. 8 men entered in yellow robes. They carried flowers, fruit and soup. They started chanting and waving flowers over him.

The room felt too full and the maharishi looked so tired.

I wanted to provide comfort for this man so I asked him, "Would you like some silence?"

He whispered, "Very much. How did you know?"

"Just by looking at you."

"Thank you for seeing. Please ask them to leave."

I went to his followers one by one and whispered, "The maharishi needs to be alone." A young man, Raj, had a shaved head with a mandala tattoo and he refused to leave, insisting he must attend to his master. But his master simply nodded at him and he left.

The maharishi fell asleep. And now I was the person who could not leave him alone. So I sat by the bed, listening to his gurgling and wheezing.

I realized I was sitting on his robe, so I folded it carefully on the table. It was so soft I kept touching it. The room smelled like the carnations placed around his head. And there was something so special about this person that I could not leave, but I stayed silent so he could sleep.

Then it was as if I could see dreams rising from his head. There were hummingbirds, their wings beating out a song like one I remembered my mother singing when I was a child.

They were flying in the night, towards the moon. A moon that grew larger until it filled the room.

I started to cry because I knew this was exactly where I should be. I'd never had that feeling my entire life. My parents divorced when I was young and I was shuttled back and forth between them. Each one made me feel as if I was just a temporary visitor, that there was no real place for me.

I felt that my whole life, no matter where I was. So even when I was living on the street it didn't feel odd, because I had no place in this world.

Only now, I did.

Now, in this room with the moon. With the silky orange robes between my fingers, and the smell of carnations and the sound of wheezing like wind through the trees.

I forgot who I was and where I was. For a moment I was a man on the moon.

Then the maharishi awoke and the moon dissolved like smoke. He opened his eyes and said, "I have been far away."

"I know, you have been on the moon."

He looked at me and said, "You saw it?"

"Yes."

He silently stared at me for so long I wondered if he'd stopped breathing. He finally whispered, "Then you must take my place when I'm gone."

"How, how can I do that?" I asked. "I know nothing."

He said, "Nothing is exactly what you need to know—And to know you know nothing. It is only by knowing nothing that we have space to discover something."

* * *

I brought him soup and fed him spoonful by spoonful.

He said, "I will die tonight, and I want you to have my robes."

"Your followers will think I've stolen them."

"Tell them you saw the moon. That is where I will go. Put on the robe now," he whispered.

I took off my clothes, shedding the last of what I used to own. I put on the robe. It was so soft, light, yet warm. They made me feel like I was inside of an animal.

He looked at me, nodded, then closed his eyes.

I sat there wondering how I ended up being exactly where I needed to be.

Suddenly the room was freezing. There was steam coming from his mouth as he breathed. I watched the steam make shapes. A whale. A dragon. A mouse. The mouse crawled across the air towards me, waiting at my nose.

I inhaled and it was part of me.

He coughed and opened his eyes slightly. He whispered so faintly I had to move closer. "Go out and do the unnecessary."

Two tiny white moons appeared in his eyes. His wheezing stopped. Then I felt as if his breath was coming out of me.

I was calm. No longer confused or afraid. I leaned in and kissed his forehead. He tasted like orange on my lips.

I walked out of the room slowly. His followers lined the hallway. Sitting, cross legged, in their yellow robes.

When they saw me, they looked afraid, then angry. Raj, who was tracing the lines of the tattoo mandala on his head stopped and jumped up.

"How dare you wear my master's robe!"

I said, in a whisper, "I saw the moon."

He fell to his knees. I'd only whispered but they'd all heard. And even though I had no idea of where to go, I trusted that wherever I went would now be where I was meant to be.

Raj said, "I would like to see him."

"He's not there. The only way is forward." I walked down the hall and heard them following me.

Raj pointed the other direction. "Sir, we must go this way." I stopped and said, "No, there is nothing we must do, except the unnecessary."

It was not necessary for me to start humming, so I did. The others joined me, randomly, at first, the various frequencies playing against each other, creating a wave of vibration. I watched everyone slow as the sound inhabited them.

Then they all stopped until only their eyes moved, watching the moon come floating down the hallway.

It wasn't necessary to create music, but it is what lets us see the moon.

Who we Were

I thought I'd get to heaven but you never know. I always tried to be a good man, kind, honest.

But I wasn't perfect. I ate meat. I gave it up for a while when we were in India. But even though I liked it and it made me feel better to eat it, it also made me feel guilty.

I mean, what if God *was* a cow? They revere them in India, so that could have been a deal breaker.

I spent my life doing good work—the peace corps, soup kitchens, nonprofits. But maybe altruism was selfish, I did it because it felt good and it made me feel less guilty.

I had the ten commandments tattooed on the souls of my feet, one tablet on each foot. I only had to take off my sandals to remind me of them—even though I knew them by heart.

Then there was the matter of my being gay, but, of course, that wasn't a decision. It just was.

When I was 14 my father screamed, "you'll burn in hell, Dennis," before he threw me out of the house and onto the street. I always thought he was wrong but I couldn't know for sure.

Douglas, my partner of 35 years, was, like me, always active in the church, but there were plenty of otherwise good folks who not too secretly thought we were going to hell for sure.

I met Douglas when we were both kids and his family's farm was just across the river. He was four years older and I always looked up to him. Then when he was 12, his family moved to Dallas and I missed him even though I told myself I didn't.

But God works in mysterious ways, and we met again 16 years later, in Niger, me in the corps and he as a missionary.

One night, lying in the desert of the Aïr Mountains, we looked into each others' eyes and just knew, and since that day we were rarely apart.

He was by my side the last 9 months when I was dying of lung cancer. Every day, he was there, reading books for me—books I had written—so that I might remember what I used to be like. I could still feel what it was like to be us.

But now we were apart.

Heaven surprised me.

All I could see were green rolling hills and farms that looked like Orange, New Jersey, when I was a kid.

It was such a glorious day. The air, sweet. And I could breathe easily at last.

The first person I saw was St. Peter. He said, "Hello! We've been looking forward to having you!"

He was so friendly, not at all austere or antique. I thought he'd be wearing a long white robe, but he was wearing a gray striped hoodie and sweatpants, like Doug used to wear.

He said, "You surely have questions."

I didn't even have to ask.

"This is how heaven looks to you, for now, so you'll feel comfortable. Don't try to figure it out, just enjoy."

And I did. Standing on my feet instead of lying in bed. The sun directly on my skin instead of through a window. The smell of wet grass and the sound of leaves rustling instead of taxis and buses.

He pointed to a big red barn and said, "You must be hungry, go, eat."

I felt the grass between my toes. I was barefoot and it felt so warm and soft and wet. The barn was just like the one across the river at the Raymeyer's farm, Doug's family.

Inside, it was spotless, and there was a buffet as long as a car, with all my favorite foods, mac and cheese with bacon, BBQ ribs with a whiskey glaze, potato salad with olives. And Waldorf salad, with mini marshmallows. All smelling just the way they did when Doug and I would have a picnic.

Standing next to the food was Martha Stewart. We used to watch her show religiously and here she was, well, perhaps not in the flesh, but here nonetheless.

"I made this all for you, Dennis," she said, smiling in that stern yet loving aunt-like way of hers.

"How did you know? and why are you here?" I asked again, because, surely, she had better things to do than cook for me, there must be millions of people entering heaven every day, she couldn't possibly keep up.

"It's my pleasure," she said, her smile genuine.

I hadn't eaten solid food in so long. I picked up a plate and started to fill it—but not too much, I didn't want to commit the sin of gluttony and be sent down to hell my very first day here.

St. Peter said, "It's OK, Dennis, you eat all you want now."

I piled my plate like it was the fourth of July, surprised that there was food here.

Then I sat on a picnic table, looking through the barn doors as the clouds sculpted the light.

I bit down on the corn on the cob. Oh, my... Corn had always been my favorite food and this, this was, dare I say "heavenly?" It yielded gently to my bite, bursting forth with buttery sweetness and leaving none of those annoying hard pieces between my teeth.

Then, after many bites of bliss, I tasted a little salt, and was reminded of Doug, and that he wasn't here to enjoy this.

I wanted him to be here—but I knew he had more to do in life, I wanted him to live it. I could wait. I told him that, silently, and hoped that he could hear.

I prayed my passing was as much of a relief to him as it was to me. That he was over the tears of sadness and onto tears of joy.

For a moment, I felt both kinds of tears at once as I tasted the salt in my mouth—bitter at having to leave Doug, and savory, for having been released from the prison of my body.

Then something in my pocket vibrated and chirped like a bird. I reached in and there was a cell phone, pearlescent but familiar.

I answered, and heard a voice I hadn't heard for so many years. My mother. "Hello,

Denny," she said softly, and the tears poured from my eyes without my even knowing I was crying.

"Do you feel ready to see me?" she asked, sheepishly. We had not left on good terms when my father threw me out of the house. Then he died and she was alone and I never forgave her. How was I allowed in heaven without having ever forgiven her?

But now there was nothing to forgive. She was only 28, he was older and always told her what to do.

She'd always been there for me before, but if he told her not to call or write me, she couldn't go against his wishes.

Then I saw her, right outside the barn doors, standing barefoot in the grass, looking all of the 14 she was when I was born—sweet, scared.

How old was I now? 67, as I was when I passed?

No, my hands looked smooth and firm and my legs felt strong like when I used to run from dad. But I was still older than she was.

She jumped on me, her arms and legs wrapped around me, not ending at our skin but melding in a way I never felt during life. Like we were one again.

She cried, "I'm sorry, baby," and I said, "I'm sorry, momma."

I saw what a girl she was—I'd only ever seen as my mother. How beautiful! How beautiful she was, smelling like peaches. She always loved peaches.

She took my hand—I could feel hers but I couldn't feel mine.

"We'll do better next time," she whispered to me, from her lips to my ears.

It reminded me when I went to see her in her later years. She had early onset Alzheimer's, and I wished I could tell her I still loved her. But she didn't know who I was. She just whispered in my ear, "Where's the potato salad?"

Then, at my feet, appeared Shirley, a golden retriever pit mix I had when I was 8. She saved me from being hit by a car then later was hit by one herself. She was so clean and didn't smell at all. She licked my feet and the three of us ran down the hill, effortlessly.

There, in the kind of gazebo I always wanted if we'd ever been able to afford a house in the country, were familiar faces. Aunt Ruth and Uncle Arthur. She with her accordion and him ready to sing.

Grampa Iggy and Gramma Helen. Lived in Florida and had a big Cadillac and here they were, in their pastel clothes and big glasses. They were all old like I remembered them.

They circled around, me in the center, touching and melting into each other like when Doug's paint would run, except that it felt totally normal here.

Then I saw myself, not a day over 20, reaching my hands out to me, and me, moving to take them.

I saw momma, nodding, and I melted through the group to myself—but it wasn't me—it was my father. We had always looked alike even if inside we were so different.

I always hoped the old man would go to hell, but here he was, he must have done something right.

"I was wrong," he said, and for a moment I felt the old anger and wanted to say, "obviously," but held my tongue, the way I always did around him, only this time it felt right. There was no need to tell him what he already knew.

"Come with me," he said, touching me. It felt oddly like holding my own hand.

Now the world started to fade, as if it had never really been there, and I was seeing a different side of heaven.

Not clouds, no angels, just a brightness that blurred all edges, even my own.

And in that infinite brightness, I could sense Doug and hear him sobbing.

I reached out through the white fog to touch him, and this time it was me feeling like I was melding with him, for an instant.

I saw him look up and knew he could sense me, too. In that instant I sent him all the love I ever had in my life.

Then I was gone. Dad and momma and everyone I knew, they were still around me, but they didn't need bodies. Neither did I.

They had been illusions. Who we were is who we always would be.

Embroidered

It wasn't my idea. I didn't want to go. It was afternoon, already getting dark early, and I was finishing the books.

Miss Lissa showed me the brochure with bright letters that said, "See Peru!"

So I looked at Peru in the brochure, put it aside and double checked the list of numbers.

Then I carefully straightened the edges of all the papers so they were like one straight, crisp line, put them in the manila folder and carried them back to my room where they would be safe.

At dinner, Miss Lissa was so animated—her hands moving as if she was yelling. She told the others, "Anna is going!"

I dropped my spoon into my soup I was so shocked.

"Where am I going?" I signed. What was happening? Why was I being forced to leave? I did good work here. I was good-natured, not easily upset like Suzanne. Not prone to shoplifting like Alan.

"I am not going anywhere," I signed. The others did not seem to care one way or another, tonight was roast chicken night and they wanted to make sure they got the parts they wanted. I liked the wing, with hard little tomatoes. I could remember at home, as a girl, holding into the wing.

But I did not get the wing. It was Delia who got it as I was signing to Lissa. I did not eat anything that night. Finally, she pointed to my room and I followed.

I could not argue with Lissa, this was her house, not that she owned it, but she was the oldest one here and had been here the longest and we all deferred to her. But she did not have the power to tell me to leave, did she?

She was sitting on my bed, not the chair. It was my bed and I did not like her sitting on it. She patted the covers and I sat next to her, unhappily. I did not like anyone in my room, much less on my bed.

She pointed to the stack of papers. Had I done something wrong? She pushed the top half of papers aside, they were no longer neat —then she pointed to the colorful brochure.

"You kept it, you want to go." she signed. I didn't like the way she signing—too broad and busy for my tastes, it was upsetting.

"I didn't mean to," I replied, feeling cold.

"But you did. You must go while you can."

I didn't move. I did not have to go. Did I? Could she make me? No, I saw no records of that happening before. Steven left to live with his family in upstate New York. Brianna moved to a home in Florida because it was warmer. But those were their decisions, at least that's what their forms said.

I just shook my head. Why was she doing this?

She signed, "Anna, you are 56 years old, if you don't do this now you may never leave this room."

Now my hands were icy but agitated—I did not like to look harsh but I was trembling. "I like like like this room," I signed—for emphasis.

"It's just a room," she signed back, smaller now, sadness in her eyes. "If I had not left where I was then I would not be here now."

"But I am am am here now. I do not need to go," I signed.

"You can always come back," she signed.

"Why go if I will come back?"

"Where are you, Anna? Where?" She was making no sense.

"I am at 1790 Grand Concourse, The Bronx, the Catholic Society Guardian Home. Have you started to forget?" I asked, touching her hand gently, because I remembered when Benitta had started to forget and her hands would move but none of us could tell what she was trying to say. It was horrible.

Lissa looked stern. "I know where I I I am, Anna. I asked where you you you were."

"I am safe here," I signed, wearily.

"That is the problem," she signed.

I thought about what she had said. All night. I looked at the gray plaster ceiling and I thought. My fingers ran across the rough sheets. I would watch for the light of dawn to trickle down through the air shaft. I looked forward to it because I was awake most every night.

Why should I go? Why? I could lie awake all night here, so why do that somewhere else?

In the morning I washed myself and went to the breakfast table. There was no one there. I had forgotten it was Sunday and they were at church. I could have gone, like I always did, but it was too late.

I did not pray. I stopped praying as a child when the Virgin Mother refused to give my hearing back. She would not even sign back to me. How could she, of course, she was just painted wood. But it was a sign she could not sign, or help me.

So from then on I would go and look at the colors in the window, and the people's faces and I would smell their winter coats and the scents on their hands and know what they had made for breakfast.

Today, in this gray kitchen I had known for 27 years, I knew everything. Every smell. Every sight. I even know what Alan and Suzanne and Lars would sign if they were here, eating their oatmeal. Nothing.

I only missed church so I could see people other than them. Each week I would sit in a new place on the pew and didn't know who would sit next to me or how they would look or smell.

Alan said I was antisocial, as if he wasn't a sociopath himself—he loved to kill spiders, while I would put them in a glass and take them outside.

This morning, with them gone, I could make whatever I wanted. I did not have to have oatmeal. I could scramble some eggs, something we only did on special occasions. I liked eggs.

I went to the refrigerator to get one, I would clean up before they were back so they would not know.

When I closed the door I was so startled to see Lissa standing there I almost dropped the egg. She had caught me.

Then she smiled, and got a frying pan, and together we made eggs, four of them, and we put sardines in them, like this was a holiday, and she did not interrupt this with signing.

The eggs were splendid. Why did I only allow myself to have them on festive days? Why did I punish myself? The car accident when I was a child that made me deaf was not my fault. I was lost in my own world, remembering, until Lissa gently tapped my shoulder.

Then we cleaned up, and opened the window. Even though it was January and cold, she lit a match for the smell and waved it.

I watched the smoke drift out the window.

"I will go," I signed to her.

"Why?" she asked me.

"To see something new," I signed.

Then, suddenly, everything felt new. A suitcase! I hadn't had one since I moved here. My clothes looked different in it. I shut it but didn't close the latches.

I opened the bottom drawer, moved an old sweater and uncovered the yellowed tissue paper. I hadn't touched this in so long and I rarely even thought about it.

But now I unfolded it on the dresser. A white handkerchief, with blue flowers embroidered on it. My mother embroidered them with her own hands. When I was younger I would run my fingers across them, like the way I saw Theresa reading braille, and I would try to feel a message in them.

The handkerchief was all I had left of my mother. She never had much. We shared a room for the last years of her life, and when she was gone I moved here.

I folded it, carefully, holding it to my nose, trying to get a faint remembrance of her. Then I put it in the lapel pocket of my gray wool blazer. I couldn't leave it behind, and I would feel safer knowing she was looking out for me.

Everyone on the trip was deaf, so I did not feel alone. I had never been in an airplane. It smelled dirty and cramped, but I loved that I could feel the movement all the time—the shaking and buzzing, and most excitingly, feeling the going up and coming down. I loved that feeling, I would sometimes take the #4 train to Grand Central just to ride skyscraper elevators and feel it, but now I was sitting down and it was such a grand feeling.

I was very tired when we reached Lima. It was so beautiful from the sky, all those red roofs and parks and circles, like so many Columbus Circles.

The hotel was old. My room was small but had windows looking out on a garden.

Everything was different. But the food. Oatmeal for breakfast. The place was different but we all looked the same.

We set off by foot down the quaint streets while our guide signed to us about the history of the city. But I was too busy looking to watch him.

There was one window filled with embroidery—scarves, dresses, lamp shades. Not just blue like my mother's flowers, but a riot of colors. I wanted to feel them.

I went inside and an old woman came up to me and smiled. I started to sign, then realized she would not understand me, so I used my voice, something I so rarely did. Then I remembered she wouldn't understand this, either.

So I touched a particularly beautiful scarf, then my heart, and I smiled, hoping she would understand.

She smiled and pointed to my mother's handkerchief, then to herself.

I nodded.

She closed her eyes and ran her fingers across the blue blossoms. When she looked up her eyes were moist.

She nodded her head, took the beautiful scarf and put it around my neck.

I shook my head as if to say, "No, I cannot afford this," then she pointed to her heart, then mine, and while I did not want any misunderstanding, somehow I knew there wasn't.

I ran my fingers across the colorful flowers, red, green, blue, orange, purple, and I felt tears in my eyes.

The flowers told me something, not words, but a feeling, like when I touched my mother's handiwork.

The woman smiled and nodded and then her hands started to move. She was signing! I did not understand what she was saying, of course, as she was signing Spanish.

When I was young I believed that if I had to be deaf, at least I could speak sign language. Unlike hearing people, who couldn't speak the languages of other countries, I could speak to deaf people anywhere.

Then I learned in school that "American" sign language was just that, American. Unlike hearing people who could understand English in Great Britain and Australia, the deaf people there had an entirely different form of sign language. Even the alphabets were different.

But somehow I understood this lady's most basic signs from the heart, and I understood it when she touched my hand with her tiny, soft fingers.

I followed her to the silent workroom in the back where she waved her hands and everyone stopped sewing. She signed them something, pointed to me, and they all put down their work and swarmed around, smiling, and reaching out their hands.

They were small people, dark, and quite beautiful. Young and old, both, and I could feel the kindness in their hands.

One by one they took me to their tables and showed me their work. I used the few signs I learned before I left to say "Thank you," and even "beautiful" which at first made a young woman laugh. The old woman who had met me, I did not even know her name, touched her mouth and smiled—and I realized I had said her work looked "delicious."

I felt myself laugh—I hadn't felt that in so long, and they laughed too.

The room was so full of color—walls of threads like the rainbow, and their hands and needles, like God's hands, making flowers grow.

I did not notice it grow dark outside. I did not worry about going back to the hotel. Everything was new. The smells, so earthy and warm, the faces, so open and happy.

They took me upstairs to where they lived. Every room had huge colorful paper flowers in them. It was so beautiful—delicious.

As was the smell, as Mary, that's what I called the old woman, led me to the dining room, a long table covered with foods I didn't know—except for a chicken, that was the same. I had seen these foods in restaurant windows but never tasted them, all the rich reds and browns and smells of spices.

She sat me at the head of the table, the guest of honor, I supposed, and they all waited. I said grace, using the only words of theirs I knew, more like telling a story with my hands, pointing to heaven, my heart, to all of them.

Then my hand flew to my mouth as I started to weep, and I saw their concerned faces through my tears.

I pointed to my tears, then to my smile. I signed a smile, and they understood—tears of joy.

Everything was different.

The food was all so delicious. Why had I never stopped at those exotic restaurants I passed?

But now, with every bite, it wasn't just the taste, but the feeling of being connected to the food, not just eating it. Sitting at this table not just next to these beautiful people, but with with with them.

After dinner a young man played the piano and I could feel the vibrations as we swayed and touched each other's hands.

Mary led me to a room with a high ceiling and windows that overlooked the city—the lights shining off the stone streets, while a lone man washed them down with a hose and broom.

My room of 27 years only had a view of brick. Here, the city sparkled.

The sheets felt soft and smelled sweet. There was no constant rumbling from the fan on the roof.

It was—delicious.

The next thing I knew I felt the sun on my eyelids. I leapt from the bed and looked outside at the golden city, pushcarts and flowers and from the kitchen the smell—of eggs.

And at the table, happy faces, and kind smiles, and eggs the likes of which I had never tasted. A young woman pointed outside the back window to the chickens.

As they went to work, I signed to Mary that I must go.

I opened my purse and took out money to pay for the beautiful scarf, but she pushed it away, then reached out her arms.

I moved to her, and felt her arms wrap around me and mine around her. When the embrace ended, I tried to ask her why, why had she taken to me.

She shook her head, not understanding. I raised my shoulders and arms.

Her face lit up. She pointed to me. She pointed to herself. She pointed down her body to her midsection, then pointed with one hand to me and the other to her. I understood.

We were sisters. She kissed my cheeks and put the scarf around my neck.

As I walked down the street to the hotel, everything was different, deliciously so. The way my feet fell on the stony street. The way the air felt, moist and warm. The smell of the buildings and flowers.

At the hotel, our guide looked angry. "Where have you been, we have been so worried!" he signed furiously.

"I was just down the street at the embroidery workshop," I signed back, calmly.

"We are all going there later today, if you had just waited for us. You must stay with the group or you will get lost!"

He took me back to the dining room. Everyone was eating oatmeal. They were wearing gray and black. It smelled like ammonia.

I went up to my room and put everything back in my bag. I walked out the front door, turned left, and walked down the street to the embroidery shop. The sign said, "Bordado Sordos," but my heart felt, "Home."

Plastic Glasses

I had a dream whilst napping when the line shut down, as it does with some regularity throughout my 12 hour shift, like when the power goes out, or there is a disruption in the supply chain. I take those opportunities to get some sleep but today I had a disturbing vision.

I was in California—I have seen it in movies on the DVDs we share at the dormitory. I have always wanted to go there, maybe live there if I could avoid getting shot on the street as so many are. I saved up and bought a t-shirt that says "California" on it with a sunset and sometimes I sleep in it so maybe that is why I was having this dream.

I was at a party, a celebration, a kind of which I did not understand—a job promotion perhaps. Everyone was big and loud and there was so much food. It was like being in an American movie, and at first I was so happy. I did not know how I got here, but maybe I had a Mustang car outside to drive, I would like that.

I went into the kitchen, which was bigger than the rooms I share with four other factory workers. A large table was covered with the plastic glasses I make. They were filled with champagne as intended. I have never had champagne and I cannot imagine what it must taste like, so I took a sip—but it just tasted like ginger ale to me. Maybe that is what it tastes like.

I remember thinking that champagne is a boring color. I like bright colors. In my room I fill the glasses with coloured water and put

them in my small window so they make the
room less gray. I am given 20 glasses a week
—the ones that aren't quite right, and I make
many things with them. I made a chandelier
of sorts, over 200 glasses I collected, strung
together with wire I took with permission
from the recycling bin. It makes the light bulb
sparkle and look special, but it also gets
dusty and is hard to clean.

Now all the big Americans came into the
kitchen and picked up the glasses and were
laughing and shared a toast. We learned how
to toast at the factory so we could know what
our customers did with the glasses. When we
have birthdays we can purchase ginger ale
and cup cakes and toast with the glasses,
clinking them and laughing when the line
has broken down.

But this was different—everything was so
loud. They were not careful, they would clink
the glasses and the champagne would spill
all over the floor and onto my shiny black
shoes—the kind of which I see in the shop
window and want to buy but do not know
where I would wear.

I saw a woman take one sip, then throw the glass into the trash—after just one sip! I never throw mine away, I wash them and make new things with them and trade them with my cousin SuLin for shoe laces and her friend TamLi for t-shirts that came out wrong.

But at this party, nothing seemed to matter, not even the glasses. They fell on the floor and people stepped on them with their big sports shoes, like the kind my brother Wiin makes—the glasses made horrible crunching sounds and became lodged in the carpet, like from the factory where I used to work in Nanyang.

The people kept getting louder—they were singing now, at a karaoke machine that's made near where my parents used to live before they were forced to sell their house. The Americans were singing strange songs, terrifyingly loud.

One man held his iPhone—I had never seen one in person even though ChinMa once worked 12 hours a day molding the round plastic button on the bottom. I have one of those buttons which I traded 10 glasses for. I keep it in my pocket—dreaming someday it might, like a seed, grow into an iPhone.

The man made music come out of the Sony speakers like they make in the Shenzhen factory where there was the chemical spill. I once had coffee with a girl who worked there. She had lost all her hair but she had a shapely skull and still looked pretty, not that I could afford to woo her.

The Americans kept getting louder, singing these songs I didn't understand, even though I am studying English, I do not know what a "camel toe" is or the meaning of "bite me." And although I understand the word "fuck" to be the obscene name for copulation, something I have never done, I did not understand song about "fuck me softly," because the whole concept is alien.

Their eyes were red—like they were becoming monsters, and they were shouting and gyrating. I have just learned that word and they were doing this and I was frightened. I was looking for the door so I could leave but I could not find it because the house was so big. I would go from room to room and there would be more people singing and drinking right out of the bottle, something I have been warned since childhood spreads disease.

I did not understand how this was happening, or why, I just wanted to leave.

I went into one room, it was all pink, and there were so many stuffed animals. Beanie Babies were the first products I ever made, when I was 9, and I still have one I found in the dumpster because his face was sewn upside down. I love that one but they didn't care about any of them—and something was moving under them and I was afraid they had come alive! The Beanie Babies fell to the floor, revealing a naked couple locked in an embrace and I slammed the door and ran.

Then I was back in the kitchen and people were dropping more plates and glasses and didn't care if they broke. Everywhere I looked were things I had once made, or were made by my friends and family, and they were all being tossed, trampled, broken, and simply thrown away in a garbage can that kept getting bigger.

I started to cry—all these things—I wanted all these things and I couldn't have them and they were being discarded so casually. I ran to get bits and pieces but they didn't matter anymore, they were worthless. Everything I had made was in the trash.

And, while I was peering down into the garbage can, someone came up from behind me, picked me up, and dropped me in. I didn't feel broken, I didn't feel useless, but there I was, among the garbage.

That is when I awoke because the line started again. 10,000 glasses an hour, that is how many I inspect. They go by on the line very fast, and I am adept at grabbing the ones that are crooked or imperfect in some way.

I do not have to be in the hot molding room with the bad smells, or the dusty pellet room, or the stifling shipping area.

It is an excellent job.

Wayne Complains

"I would have made a lousy pioneer," Wayne admitted as if I could possibly be surprised by this. Wayne was the most delicate person I'd ever met. He was always either too hot or too cold, too hungry or too full. Too tired or too wired.

He was always complaining, yet somehow in such a sweet way that I didn't mind. In fact, I looked forward to it. What won't be right for Wayne today or this hour or this minute?

It was always something new, like "these socks are scratchy." Oh, what an interesting revelation as I'd never experienced scratchy socks myself. Or "my teeth feel slimy." Slimy teeth? Is that even a thing? Well, it was for Wayne.

Everything was a thing for Wayne and while I'm sure that might have annoyed the fuck out of some people it delighted me.

Because what it said to me was that Wayne could feel *everything*. Literally everything. "I smell onions," he'd announce while we were in the middle of the forest. How could there be onions in the forest that only Wayne could smell?

Did he have the sensory abilities of a bloodhound? In fact, yes. We discovered a camper grilling onions after tromping around for a while, but only after Wayne complained about mosquito bites. The bites bothered me, but not the way they annoyed him where it seemed to occupy every beat of his heart, every wavelength of his brain until he had to do something about it.

This was the other thing that impressed me about Wayne is he'd always do something about it. If he announced, "I'm too hot," he would drop his clothes. He'd rather be mostly naked, then too hot. Even in a public place, he thought nothing of shedding his shirt, or even pants, exposing his bony body in boxers.

He never went beyond the bounds of propriety, at least in public, but Wayne was quite happy being naked, unless there were mosquitoes, in which case he wore something of his own making that was not unlike a beekeeper's outfit, including gloves and netting over his head.

I wondered how he ever had the bandwidth to do anything else in his life, other than take care of his immediate reactions to everything, "This coffee is too hot for my tongue... This ice is too cold on my fillings..."

And yet, Wayne had a magic way with numbers. I've never understood numbers—odd abstract symbols. I didn't understand how they worked together, the way colors do.

But for Wayne, numbers combined like they were having passionate sex. He'd stare at them and I'd see the smile on his face. This was after taking off his socks or rubbing a bite or massaging his hand, which was prone to... what is it called when your eyelid shakes with that quivering... whatever it's called, his hand did that. I could see it happen on the fine skin of his hands, almost translucent. We used to joke about his "semi albino" skin. He didn't care—he was too excited by numbers and the possibilities of what they could do.

He'd studied theoretical mathematics and worked as a consultant for Rand, taking in these projects which literally made no sense to me whatsoever. To me they were a jumble of random marks on a page.

Yet he'd get very excited, sometimes erotically, I could see it growing in his pants, and I'd ask, "What, what do you see there?" He explained to me—He was seeing the universe in action. The purity of time and space, and matter and mass. All revealing themselves to him.

It made me jealous. I wanted to be able to see that. I want to be able to feel everything! Feel anything.

I was supposed to be the artist of us two. I painted my watercolors, which everyone said were beautiful. I had no problem selling because they were pretty but to me they were only pretty. Looking at one of my pictures you could never feel an itch, sense the roughness of socks, or fear the scent of a nearby bear.

That's precisely what Wayne said he loved about my paintings. When he stared into them, sometimes, for an entire minute, he wouldn't be too hot or cold, or have a headache that I could somehow feel along with him as it went from the top of his head down his spine to his toes.

His headaches got worse. His twitches, that's the word, "twitches," got more severe in his hands and his shoulders, in his lower back, in his thighs. The worse it got, the less control he had over everything, including his own body, yet the less he'd complain. I worried for him, "Are you too hot, too cold? Can I get you something to drink? Are you hungry?"

He sat three feet away from a wall which I painted like a forest so that he had something beautiful to look at. He'd sit there for an hour and only occasionally say something like, "I smell a campfire." Only there was no campfire. Not there in his hospital room.

"I hear an owl," he whispered to me, staring at the painting. No mosquitoes. No fear of an approaching bear.

Peace. That's what I was able to give him in his final days.

And he gave me the ability to feel, even if only never ending grief.

Now when I go to the forest to paint, I'm consumed by the itch of mosquito bites.

Monkey glyphics

I ce cream sandwiches. That was the only thought in my mind as I left the house just after midnight. This had happened before, only last time it was for Double Stuf Oreos, which turned out to be so greasy and disgusting that I almost gave them to a homeless man before it dawned on me that if I did I'd get home with nothing.

So I headed down Prager Parkway to the aging mini-mall of my youth, now almost completely surrounded by a chain link fence with signs saying, "Coming soon..." That's all, just "Coming soon..." not a picture of a new mall or anything else.

I walked in through the driveway, which had a gate that was always open, and headed to the LUCKY Supermarket whose sign now read, "UCKY" as the "L" had burned out.

Inside the place lived up to its new name. Half the fluorescent lights were out, the other half flickered like in a zombie movie. The floor was covered with salmon-scented pools of especially slippery water.

I thought this was very cool, I mean, normally you have to wait till October and pay a lot to go to a place like this. I fully expected some faux-undead employee to jump out at me screaming "brains!" I'd feel superior because I'd know it was just some high-school kid, paid minimum wage to scare me and I wasn't falling for it, so they'd be disappointed, and undead.

As long as I was here I figured my mom would want some half-and-half, because she was always saying to me, "Teddy, get momma some half-and-halfsky." That's what she called it, mixing it with Vodka to make her own special concoction she called "mother's milk."

She'd sip it with a straw while watching anything on TV, literally anything, most often infomercials about makeup that promised to revitalize her youth. Then a week later a box would arrive with a name like, "YouthGlow!" and would sit there on the porch until I brought it in and opened it to find a jar the size of a peanut butter cup and a receipt that had to be wrong because there was no way this thing could cost $125. Then I'd call the credit card company and claim someone had stolen her card, again, get the charge reversed, then add the jar to her collection of unopened jars that had the word "youth" on them in gold letters.

So there I was, where the dairy section used to be—and there was an old brown couch facing a sea of empty shelves. My immediate thought was, "Not my fault," and I fell into the sofa because while all this was cool, it was exhausting waiting for an undead teenager to pop out, which had yet to happen.

I checked my phone to see if anyone had bought tickets to my Fringe show, "Mother May I?" my one-man show about growing up with an alcoholic mother and an abusive if mostly absent father who I suspected had another family he liked better a few blocks away. I once went up and down the streets of my neighborhood and saw a car that looked like his at another trailer. I knocked on the door and a nice woman in an apron opened the door, as the smell of apple pie wafted out from behind her.

"Is my father here?" I asked, tired, because I was pretty much always tired, as was everyone else I knew.

"No, honey, why would your daddy be there?" She smiled like a lady in a soap commercial.

"'Cause that's his car in the driveway," I explained.

"No, honey, that's my Mustang, pretty, ain't it?"

I looked into the car window and it was clean inside with a plastic daisy growing out of the cup holder. The cup holder in my father's car was filled with cigarette butts. Maybe she wasn't lying. The license plate said, "PIE LADY," which is definitely not what my father's said.

"I'm sorry, pie lady, my mistake."

"That's perfectly alright, young man. I just took an apple pie out of the oven if you'd like a slice."

I thought about it, then heard my father's voice say, "Strangers will lure you into their houses, offer you something sweet and drugged, fuck you in the ass and kill you." I turned around and nobody was there, so I guess once again he was talking into my head.

I smiled back at her, "Thank you, lady, but I'm... apple intolerant," I said before turning and running away as fast as I could.

That story was in my Fringe show, which, if the ticket website was to be believed, had sold zero tickets to my three shows. That was so surprising to me, my one-man-show-coach 3J (Jennifer Jane Jackson) said she "promoted you tirelessly to my large mailing list to ensure maximum sales," or so her full-color three-fold brochure promised. I'd already paid her $375 to rent the theater, sure I'd earn that back and be seen by a talent agent who'd get me my own sitcom.

I heard about 3J through my friend Lila, who had her one-woman show about growing up with an abusive father and an alcoholic mother. Lila's show moved me, and the two other people in the audience who were also creating their own deeply felt one-person shows. We laughed, we cried. We wondered if we could use any of her stories in our own shows (Jennifer said, "of course!").

Lila got a review on the Fringe site, written by Jennifer. "A revelation! Lila is luminous as she spins tales of surviving a desperate youth!"

Jennifer introduced me to Miles who designed my poster, a picture of me photoshopped holding an alligator, which wasn't in the show but which he said would be "arresting.' It prominently featured Jennifer's quote for me, "A miracle! Ted is tumultuous as he spins tales of surviving a desperate youth!"

I felt so good about my show and the poster and all. It was a much better use of my Burger King earnings than buying a car.

But I was disappointed that nobody had bought a ticket in the past hour, or the two weeks since sales started. I texted Lila saying she needed to buy one since I bought one for her show.

I looked up from my phone, having forgotten that someone might jump out to scare me, but nobody did. Still, it did smell fishier back here, so I got up, trying to avoid the slick puddles, In the flashing gloom, I noticed the entire meat and fish section was not just cordoned off with yellow and white caution tape, but was also wrapped in large green sheets of stretch plastic as if it was containing something deadly. Cool.

Focus—I had a mission: ice cream sandwiches. So I walked gingerly to the open top freezer cases in the middle of the store. The lights were out in the cases, and the flashing fluorescents above made it hard to find anything in them so I reached for my phone to use the flashlight. Damn, I'd left my phone on the sofa. I had to tiptoe back, always on the lookout for people who might jump out and scream and was disappointed when nobody did.

Back at the freezer case... nothing was cold. In fact, it was hot and humid. And there were no ice cream sandwiches!

But there was a black and white monkey, laying face up, in the bottom of the case. I flashed my flashlight at him, because I thought he might be undead and going to scream and scare me, but no, he was breathing. Disappointed again.

He started writing a series of Egyptian-looking symbols, one that looked like an ice-cream sandwich, another a screaming monkey, then an upside-down smiley face, like the one on my hoodie.

He was reading my mind and writing my thoughts! So fucking cool! I had a flash of inspiration (the monkey drew a lightning bolt). This is exactly what my Fringe show needed (the monkey drew fringe). I needed to find the manager to ask if I could borrow the monkey (the monkey drew a man in a white coat with a nail through his head, again, cool!).

I went to where the registers were and was relieved to see a display of Almond Joy bars that were probably still edible. I put one in my pocket and then had to decide which was more important to me, to sneak out with the candy bar, or to get the monkey for my show. Maybe the monkey.

I called out, "Manager, I need a manager," and heard nothing other than hissing pipes and sparking lights. Oh, well, at least I'd get a candy bar, I thought as I headed out the door, only to be blocked by a large man in a white coat. He didn't have a nail in his head, the monkey must have taken artistic license. I loved that monkey!

"Where do you think you're going with that Almond Joy?" he asked menacingly, but not nearly as scary as he could have done it.

I lied, "I left my wallet in the car and was just going out to get it," I told him. He pulled the candy from my back pocket, felt me up a little bit and said, "Go get it and come back or I'm calling the cops." Ooh, yes, undead cops, that I wanted to see!

I went to a nearby car, which obviously wasn't mine because I could only afford a 2002 Toyota Yaris in my dreams, pretended to open the door and pull out my wallet, then dutifully came back into the store, waiting for the undead cops.

The cash registers were dark, so the manager punched some numbers into the calculator on his phone. "A dollar 63," he said, wheezing.

"What happened here?" I asked, hoping he'd have a good scary story.

"Busted pipes in the coolers. It's a health hazard."

"Yeah, I'm sure, cool!" I replied, thinking $1.63 was way too much for a candy bar, but then all these special effects must have cost major coin. I counted out my nickels, dimes, two quarters and didn't have any pennies. "A dollar sixty?" I asked, as he snatched the change out of my hands.

I tore open the Almond Joy and stuffed one into my dry mouth.

"Oh," I added, momentarily unable to think of anything other than the taste of soft, sweet coconut and hard slightly-burnt tasting almonds, "Can I borrow your monkey?"

"What monkey?" the manager wheezed.

"The one in the freezer case that reads minds and writes in Egyptian."

"Hieroglyphics? Naw, it doesn't work for me, it just moved here now that the freezer case feels like the tropics."

"Do you mind if I borrow it?'" I asked.

"You'll have to take it up with the monkey," the manager said, distracted, before running off screaming, "Get out, lady, it's a health hazard!"

I went back to the monkey and asked if it would like to come with me and be in my Fringe show. It looked at me, blankly. Right, of course it didn't understand English. So I thought, "Do you want to come with me and be in my Fringe show?"

Now the monkey jotted down a picture of my hoodie, a 25 seat theater full of people, the monkey's face making a hideous scream while chasing the terrified audience. Yeah that worked for me. Then it drew an all-too-realistic sketch of my mother's trailer, complete with the scowling leprechaun out front, then a picture of the monkey taking a shower.

It reached its arms up, grabbed the collar of my t-shirt and pulled itself up, its claws only digging into me a little bit. I took that as a "yes."

We walked back to my house, and all the while I heard it eating the other half of my Almond Joy and scribbling my thoughts: a full audience, a review in the LA Times, a meeting with Netflix executives, a Netflix home screen with a featured image of me peeking out from behind a screaming monkey. Yup, my dream come true.

Inside it dragged me to the shower, and it was only when I lathered it up that I realized it was a he, hard to miss as he seemed to find my soapy body arousing. He tried to mount me, which was difficult to avoid in the small shower. I slipped and fell, only making it easier for him. I didn't want to upset him or he might not do my show. Besides, my screaming only seemed to encourage him.

"Did you get momma some half-and-halfsky?" I heard momma say, just outside the shower curtain because the bathroom door lock had stopped working ages ago.

"No, momma, they were out!" I managed to blurt between screams.

"Lazy asshole," she said. Hardly.

The Monkey was quite sweet to me after—grooming my head and pubic hair and finding a few things to eat. He shook himself dry, getting water all over the bathroom, which I wiped off with the towel, then dried myself.

Gosh, all this was tiring. The monkey took my bed and I lay on the shag carpet. I wondered what the monkey's name was. It scribbled the word "Fang." I took a picture of him, baring his teeth. Cool. I went to the Fringe website and updated my show title to "Attack of the killer monkey!!!" and replaced the picture of me with Fang's terrifying face. I showed it to him to make sure he liked it. He drew a smiley face, patted my head, then started to snore.

I stared at the ticket sale screen. Chime! One ticket sold, two, three... 16... I fell asleep, even as the chimes kept coming.

Settle in the Seat

I always had the same dream before Monte Carlo. Year after year, the same dream.

I would be rounding the turn at El Dorado—my line was perfect—but the car would shudder, and the right rear wheel would simply snap off and fly, sickeningly, into the crowd. Then I'd see *her* and wake up.

I had dreams like this before every race in every city—in Tokyo I'd dream I had food poisoning and would throw up on my seat before I could sit down. In Berlin, I would find myself in the car, drunk, and when the green flag came down I'd just sit there, unable to move. In Indianapolis it would be a horrible noise, I'd drive into the pit and they'd tell me they didn't have the part to fix it.

The dreams never came true, but they were always there.

But Monaco was the worst. Wheels could break free and fly into the crowd. What if mine killed...

It didn't make sense, I'd won Monaco three times—it was the most challenging race— through the heart of the city on roads never designed for such things, yet every time I was afraid. I told myself this was good, that the day I was not afraid of the race was the day I would die.

And so, the dreams lead me to have a list, in my head, to make the pit crew double check things. I insisted they always triple check the brakes. Most importantly, were all the wheel lugs and tyres sound, tight, no stripped threads?

I was just starting my career when I learned that lesson. I was young enough to feel invincible, and I was driving too hard. You have to drive as close to the limits of your car as you can but I would push just past them, then pull back, and it worked for a while.

I was at Brighton, in an obscenely blue Ford Cortina that stood out on the track, that's all I cared about at the time. I was taking the "Wicked" curve, notoriously tight, and was just a hare ahead of another driver. I don't even remember who he was but his car was green, I remember that.

And I held off on the brakes until, well, until too late. Because when I did hit the pedal, it collapsed onto the floorboard. There was nothing there, the fluid was all gone, and at that speed there was nothing to do but watch —the right fender hitting the concrete barrier, sparks flying. The entire right side of the car sliding against the wall, sparks, heat, burning smells. I was wearing leathers and I could feel and smell them smoking hot as the right side of the car was pressed ever closer to me.

The tyres sheared off, flying into the air—like in my later dreams but here messy, spinning, tread shearing off.

And then the car just stopped. I released my belts and jumped out as soon as I could and ran—that's what you learn—jump and run— just in case the gas tank blows, which it did, a huge ball of flame, turning that stupid blue to black.

After that I started to use techflex brake lines —they're covered in a metal, woven like cloth. I got the idea from airplanes which used them because of the changes in pressure.

And each time I'd have a problem on the track, that would be one more line item on the checklist in my head, and my crew knew the list even without my telling them, but I'd tell them anyway.

So that night, before Monte Carlo, I lay in bed waiting for that dream—the tyre flying—with me waking up before it ever landed. But it didn't come. I got so tired waiting for it I fell asleep.

And I did dream—I was swimming off the Port DuVille, not a good place to swim, too many large yachts. A fish comes swimming up to me—and it speaks—a talking Scottish salmon. The kind of thing that somehow seems normal in a dream. It says to me, "This is your last race." It was something I'd been thinking as I would turn 40 in two months time.

"Remember it," the fish said before it swam away.

And there I was, in the sea, trying to figure out why that fish said this to me. I did not usually remember races—there's no time to remember—unless something goes wrong.

I woke up, and just then my alarm went off and it startled me, so I didn't think about the dream, I thought about my race day routine.

Every driver has a routine, it's partly ritual and partly superstition. You want to do things exactly as you did them when you won a race. As if that has some magic power.

So I stood in the shower, the hot water running over me and visualized the course. I did not shave, I never shaved on race days because I once cut myself and even though it was small, during the race it started bleeding and the blood got into my eyes and I had to stop, the only time I didn't finish a race. So no more shaving.

I put on the hotel robe, got my breakfast waiting outside the door. Three eggs, soft boiled in their shell. That's all. No coffee, not after Torquay. I cracked the shells and spooned the soft egg into my mouth and thought about the chickens where I grew up and my father teaching me how to drive the tractor.

The very first day I was so excited, I'd never driven anything with a motor. I jumped in and turned the key, then pappa, very gently, turned it off. He was a gentle man, a true gentleman. And he told me how to drive, the most important advice I ever got.

"First, you must settle into the seat," he told me. It's something I did from that day forward, in every car.

I sit in the seat and put my hands down, touching the sides of the seat. I don't touch the wheel yet.

I close my eyes, and I see every piece of the car, every bolt, every screw, connector, metal panel, hose, the springs, struts, wheels, bearings, tyres, then back up to the engine, the cylinders, pistons, spark plugs—the petrol mist in the carburetor, exploding to flame in the chamber. "You are riding fire," he told me.

Then I put on my fireproof underclothes and jumpsuit. My driver is at the door—yes, I always had a driver drive me to the race—I didn't want to have street driving in my bones when I got to the track.

I talk to Alain, head mechanic. He tells me they replaced the head. I don't like new parts before a race, but he said Jaguar tested it.

Checklist with the crew—wheels, brakes, fuel, mix. Quiet—listen to the engine.

In the car—settle into the seat. This seat is narrow and bolted to the floor with thick rubber gaskets to help keep the vibration of the car from shaking me too much. I was the only one with such gaskets and I didn't tell other drivers about this until I retired. It gave me an edge—just enough separation from the machine to reduce fatigue, but still tightly part of it.

Today I closed my eyes and settled into the seat. But it's hard to imagine the entire car.

My mind keeps going back to that first day with papa, imagining huge tractor wheels instead of my racing slicks.

And I smelled... fish. Not cooked fish, but the smell when you first pull one from the sea— briny, salty, bloody.

I open my eyes and look around. Everything is as it always was.

Except—it's oddly silent. I don't hear anything but my own breath. And I'm too calm. I'm not afraid.

I see my pit boss nod. The other cars line up at the start. I release the clutch, press on the accelerator and move to join them.

I am not afraid. I'm not even worried about not being afraid. It is a bit like watching the movie they made about my life starring Steve McQueen.

I see the green flag fall, and feel my feet moving to engage the clutch and floor the accelerator. I can hear the engine rev and feel the earth roll beneath me—but something's different.

And then I see it—a flash of yellow in the stands on my right. Not just any yellow, but her yellow—she always wore yellow hats.

I don't worry about my tyres flying off. I don't even care about winning.

I am flying. Everything is so clear. I remember every single instant of it.

And then on the next lap, right in front of the stands, I see it—small, silver, in the road, moving. There is no way to swerve at this speed and I drive over it—I hear it hit the undercarriage, feel the car shake.

I smell an explosion of salmon. Cooked with motor oil on a hot engine.

And again, see yellow in the stands.

The car shudders a bit, but I keep my line.

And now all I want is a baked salmon with butter and lemon like...

But there are cars in the way—between me and... so I simply pass them, I see a line to the left or right and I take it as if I was on the expressway. I think how easy it is when it no longer matters.

I was the first across the line and I didn't care. I pulled into the pit, jumped out of the car and lay down next to it, looking for proof. There were some silver spots on the wheel well, but they could have been chipped paint —except they came off on my fingers.

I forgot about the winner's circle and the great silver cup, I just wanted to make sure this was real. The crew hovered over me, yelling, as if I'd gone insane, and I laughed and jumped up.

I felt a little dizzy, even before I saw it—the yellow hat, floating on a sea of spectators... swimming away from me.

Nothing else mattered now. I pushed my way through the crowd, towards the yellow hat. Pretty soon people backed away from the crazy driver who'd just won Monte Carlo and was running away from the winner's circle.

And as I got closer to the hat, I thought, "Maybe it's not her, maybe it's someone else, maybe I am the crazy idiot she always said..."

Then she turned around.

Annabella. Huge yellow hat over now silvering hair down to her bare shoulders.

I smelled fish again—so strong this time, as I slowly walked up to her.

She took off her large daisy-shaped sunglasses. Her eyes looked like the ocean in my dream, green and brown and silver.

I was close enough to touch her. Why did it smell so much like...

Smack, across my face, cold, wet, fishy.

I looked up to see her brandishing a silver salmon.

It slipped out of her hands as she reached around my neck—jumping into my arms.

Things I didn't do

The things I didn't do could fill a book I'll never write.

I always called myself a writer, but, in fact, I edited other writers' work. I would "make it better," which felt like "making it."

But now when I saw my hands holding a pen, I wasn't writing words, I was making red marks.

I was also very tan, as tennis was mindless and therefore preferable to thought.

September was a good month for vegetables, too, so the boinking of balls and swelling of zucchini and fragrance of fresh dirt filled my days as my words went unwritten.

"Maybe I should become a tennis pro and garden—I could create tennis gardens!" I thought, idiotically.

Anything to keep from writing.

October, a manuscript arrived from the famous Finnish author, Inge Wenge.

He wrote English the way I played tennis—mindlessly but not bad.

His words volleyed across the page, bouncing out of bounds, rolling until they lost energy and stopped.

I couldn't change a word. Not a word. Not a comma, or period or, or, or...

How dare I even touch his words, written as they were from his very soul?

Who was I to even edit?

So I didn't.

I sent it back to the publisher with thousands of red marks—every one meaningless. Yet, somehow together, they formed a portrait of the reader in the process of reading.

I told Joyce, the head of acquisition, I need to speak to Inge before he saw my notes. But it was too late. He had seen them.

I thought he'd be furious and expose me as the no-talent dilettante I felt I had become.

But he said, "I see what you are doing and all your marks must stay. Who am I to change marks that come from your very soul?"

So that is how "Wings, Water and Wind," was published.

His black words. My red marks.

It was heralded as an entirely new art form of word and image as one.

It was the only thing I could think to do.

And it was enough.

The Queen of Chabert Falls

Mother kept her necklace in the armory. It was far too precious to keep in the safe at home behind her portrait painted by some famous artist from Paris who I never got to meet. I never get to meet anyone of interest.

Legend has it that the necklace was owned by the Romanovs, and by "legend" I mean "mother's story." She didn't trust the bankers —"those people," she called them—"so many of their race are jewelers and could replace it with paste."

Nothing would do, but the armory, guarded by 1,800 able bodied men (whom I also never get to meet, thank you very much).

Besides, the pomp is just too precious—on the evening of a ball, father is sent to Fort Chabert where he informs the captain of the guard that the necklace is required by "her ladyship." I don't know why he calls her that. Just come out and say, "The Queen," which is what I call her, at least in my diary and sometimes to Mary, Celia, or Emily.

Then a top-ranking contingent of the fort's finest are sent, in full parade dress, guarding the large, flat, midnight blue silk box. They arrive at the door, exactly 22 minutes before mother and father must leave, with a ceremonial trumpeter (if one can be spared), and march in formation into the front hall.

Father leads mother by the hand, she already in her gown. The luckiest of the men kneels down and opens the box with a flourish, revealing its midnight blue velvet interior on which glows— (in no small part due to the chandelier overhead that Mary must light before this important event)—the necklace.

The necklace is the most beautiful thing I have ever seen, other than mother. I am quite envious of mother. She has always been beautiful, if not always rich.

She has exactly the life she wants—the leading lady of the leading family in these parts—even if this is not exactly Chicago or New York.

There she might be a small fish, but here, she is "The Queen of Chabert Falls"—and I am not the only one to call her that. Though I may be the only one to call her that with a mocking tone, never to her face, of course, as I do not want to incur her wrath—nobody does.

The necklace is made up of 16 perfectly matched natural Tahitians pearls which, the story goes, were taken by Commander Svenavanich, who established the Russian navy sometime. I am not good with dates.

Each time she tells the story it becomes more grand, with the Commander (I have difficulty saying his name, and mother says it differently each time, too), having killed dozens of orientals to procure the precious pearls.

Yet the pearls are only a backdrop to the real drama, 24 teardrop shaped diamonds, ranging in size from 1 carat at the small end near the clasp, to the largest, 6 carat, in the middle.

They are all white, they are all flawless, and, if mother is to be believed, they are all real. The box says "Faberge" so even I, perhaps the most cynical person in all of Chabert Falls, believes this to be true.

Somehow, as splendid as this glittering necklace is, when mother dons it, she shines brighter. It reflects light upward to illuminate her face, and refracts downward, making her décolletage radiant.

She once allowed me to try on the necklace, for my 16th birthday, though I wasn't allowed to wear it to my party. It was so huge and heavy that when I looked in the mirror all I could see was the necklace. It was as if I'd become invisible.

I am invisible to mother most of the time, but with the necklace on, I couldn't even see myself.

It fits mother like it was made for her—that's what everyone says, and in this rare case, everyone is correct.

Mother pairs it with two large pearl earrings father brought back from Holland, and a lustrous mother of pearl hair comb from Spain on which she had a jeweler add a few more pearls, just to "make it more special," she said. And it did.

Before she leaves, she expects us all to line the front hall to gaze on her beauty. She doesn't call it that, but that's how I feel. And no matter how cross I may be about the ritual, every single time I am as taken by her beauty, as father must have been 25 years ago, and still must be today.

Her hair is naturally the color of Ladyfaire roses, her skin finer than any porcelain, her eyes emerald green, and her figure—

perfection—she hardly needs a corset to show a girlish waist below her womanly bosom.

Out they sweep, to some glittering event, and I go back to my embroidery, or sometimes chatting with Emily, her lady's maid. Emily's my age, and when mother isn't here, my best friend. Yes, other young ladies my age call on a regular basis, and we sit, stiffly, and have tea and sandwiches and talk about nothing, or boys, which are mostly nothing at this age, honestly, they're still like children. Then they leave and if Emily isn't busy with mother's bath or mother's hair or mother's pedicure, I talk to her about how shallow and annoying the other girls are.

Yesterday Emily said to me, "You are not like those girls, miss, but you pretend to be, so they may think the very same thing of you that you think of them." For someone with virtually no education, she is very wise, indeed.

I took this to heart and went calling on Alexandra Cooper-Smith, a girl who, I thought, might actually be a human being underneath all those curls. I got this idea into my head because of a single look I saw her give Sally-Anne Corruthers at her birthday luncheon, as if Sally-Anne was the stupidest thing in the state, which I do believe she is.

The calling card I sent to Alexandra said I would like to go for a "spirited walk," which means "a real walk, rather than a dressy stroll." Girls at our age were not expected to walk in a spirited manner, but this was the first test to see if Alexandra might actually be up to the task of being a true friend.

I wondered what we would talk about. Mostly what I do with Emily is complain, and this did not seem appropriate for cultivating a true friendship. I had read about true friendships in books but never felt as if I'd had one, other than Emily.

And I could not talk to her about how angry I was that I was not allowed a proper education, like Robert. He was learning languages and history and I was learning... embroidery. Not even real sewing, like Emily did to make or mend some of mother's things. Nothing useful.

Just enough to make beautifully monogrammed handkerchiefs. Like every other girl. So when my birthday would come, I could expect a stack of perfectly monogrammed handkerchiefs to add to my stack from the previous year that I'd never used.

Sometimes, when I would sit with Emily, I would re-embroider them with other initials, like EM for Emily, MA for Mary, and CW for Celia. One year I gave each of the maids three handkerchiefs with their initials on them, and they were so delighted. It made me feel bad—them being so delighted by something I didn't care about at all—though I had wanted them to have something nice.

That is my other downfall. According to mother, I am "too nice." Mother never suffers from this malady. I once overheard Mrs. Wilson in town call her the "iron fist with the velvet glove" which I thought was brilliant until I also read it in a book and realized it wasn't original.

I thought of mother as something other than human. As if she was made from a cloud of diamond dust that had coalesced into human form after being hit by lightning. There was always something dangerously electrifying about her.

I thought this was all in my imagination, which can be quite vivid as I have little else to do. I said this to Emily once—in anger— then immediately regretted saying such a thing as it reflected poorly on me, and also might get back to mother.

Emily simply laughed. She said she once walked into the boudoir when mother was doing something normal, perhaps plucking an eyebrow, and mother stared daggers at her through the mirror. She said she felt like she would melt—actually physically melt!

Oddly, that made me feel a bit of compassion for mother. Perhaps her perfection was difficult to maintain, especially in complete secrecy. I never saw her speak with anyone other than the few women with enough status to call, and even then Mother was always in charge.

Perhaps it was exhausting for her not to be able to have a spirited walk with a close friend and bare her heart. It had been for me.

Do not get me wrong, Emily is a dear friend, but obviously cannot publicly be so. We cannot walk together out of doors and can only meet in her room—not even in my own room in case someone might see us.

I longed for a friend who knew what it was like to be me, to be 18 and wanting to explore the world but still not allowed to do anything on her own.

Alexandra lived only a mile down the road, so I started my spirited walk with a walk to her home. When I arrived, I was so pleased to see Alexandra wearing her tweeds as well—she understood already!

She immediately took my hand and we walked towards the woods. I liked this girl.

I told her, quite plainly, that I wanted a friend I could speak openly to, no pretense. She said she so wanted the same thing and that the other young ladies were insufferable—and made that face again. I knew I had been right about her!

I thought I was the only one to bridle at the constraints of our class, but Alexandra was far more, how shall I say, precocious than I was. She had already kissed a boy, she informed me, and it was not her fiance, one Simon Stoneman, from Milwaukee. Naturally I was thrilled by this news and wanted to know if it was different than when one practiced kissing with a maid. She said it most certainly was, as boys are not nearly as soft or smart.

And so the afternoon went, with me learning far more than I expected as Alexandra chatted away openly, and happily—filling my head with dreams.

I returned before dinner, my shoes muddy—but Celia would take care of that. I bathed and changed for dinner and, in an unusual occurrence, mother and father were already at the table when I arrived. I apologized for being late, for I felt I must have been late, but mother said I was not late and they had something to tell me.

Mother was wearing her red satin with cream lace. Father wore a black suit, but father always wore a black suit, except when dressed in his formal military uniform.

I loved to see father in his uniform, it reminded me of the story he told about meeting my mother. It was the only time I could imagine her as a real girl, like me.

He was already a Captain at Fort Wayne. She was not from a good family at all, though that's not the story she tells now. It was at the Christmas dance with a real orchestra—a big occasion in that small town.

Mother was not there to dance, no, she was arranging the food on the table, and making sure the waiters' trays were set with drinks.

Even though I know this story is true, it is hard for me to imagine mother doing anything approaching real work. Yet I know she grew up on a farm and her father died when she was 14 and she took a job at an inn to help support her mother, as she was an only child.

Still, I could not imagine a cloud of diamond dust, even a young one, serving other people.

Father said even back then she was the most beautiful girl in the room, and the other girls, in their fancy dresses, were not happy with their beaus glancing her way. Father, being an officer, did not have a belle, but was there to represent the men of the Fort as a liaison to the locals.

That's what father was always good at—and he soon left the service to work for a munitions manufacturer, again as a liaison, in Washington. He knew the business, he had contacts in the military and he was a "valuable asset."

I love that term. I have always wanted to be a "valuable asset" to something.

He soon moved up the chain of command at his company, and now, after 24 years, he is the managing director. He runs the company. And mother runs the town.

"Lilliane," my mother said in her tornado whisper, "Your father and I have something to tell you. Sit down."

I sat.

Father pulled out mother's chair and she sat, while he continued to stand, at attention.

"Your father and I have been discussing your future," she said, seeming distracted.

I felt my face get hot and my hands, too. Perhaps it was from too much walking, but I was also getting angry. Mother and father were planning my future without so much as consulting me?

"You are at an age..." my mother started, and I could not hold my tongue.

"No." was all I could say, but I said it.

Mother looked at me the way I once saw her look at the cook when she found a small piece of bone in her salmon.

"Excuse me?" she said—was her face turning red, too? Was that even possible?

"No." was all I could say, but I did say it.

Father seemed to hear it this time, and said, "Young lady…" but that's all he said.

"I am not going to marry Wilson Fredricks." I announced, with courage that came from I do not know where. The spirited walk, perhaps.

Mother glanced at father. Father did not move. I folded my hands in my lap so they could not be seen shaking.

It seemed like a very long time passed without anyone saying anything, during which time mother's face became as composed as the portrait of her at the end of the dining table, which was the one painted previous to the one in the sitting room.

"You were not asked to speak," mother said, now more queenly. "Nor did we ask for your opinion."

We. There, she's said it. It wasn't "your father and I," it was the "*royal we.*"

I should have been terrified. When she used "we" it usually meant someone was going to be fired or forced to move out of Chabert Falls or something equally awful.

I saw Emily peeking from behind the serving screen, behind my parents, smiling. She was always there as part of service but, being a girl, was not allowed to be seen serving.

Her smile emboldened me, though I knew I was already past the point of no return.

"You are getting too old to play at home like a child. And, Emily, I hear you moving behind the screen and know you must have been the one to tell Lillianne, so you will be relieved of your position, post haste."

I heard Emily gasp and leave.

And that was it. That was the moment I saw her facade of diamond dust was only that—a facade. I saw the girl from the poor family, trying furiously to retain her composure—and control. Trying to secure my future to be like hers.

Rather than being angry with her, I felt sad—how did she become like this? Was father lonely? Was she?

Now that her spell had been broken, I got up from the table and walked to her. I touched her cheek—it was flesh, hot, and she flinched away from me.

"Mother, I have always wished I could be like you, but now, I wish you could be like me."

She looked stunned, as if she'd been awoken from a lovely dream by a wild animal that had somehow found its way into her home.

Father simply looked uncomfortable, and announced, "I will let you two ladies sort this out," turned on his heels as if in a military parade, and left.

Mother's face was now as red as her hair, something I had never seen. I kneeled next to her and took her hand which reminded me of an orchid.

"I have always wanted to be like you—to know what I want. But I do not, mother."

I waited for her to speak but she was silent. Her eyelids flitted as if she was thinking in Morse code.

I spoke, plainly, "Today Alexandra told me that the Army is looking for young women to be nurses."

Mother's mouth opened, briefly, as if she was going to speak, then closed again.

"I decided I am going to Fort Wayne to learn to be a nurse."

"But..." mother said, then stopped.

"I am happy for you, mother, because you seem happy here. I simply want to be happy myself, somewhere."

Mother's hand grasped mine, hard, I had no idea she had such a strong grip. Her other hand was on the table, and I couldn't help but wonder if it was moving towards a knife. But then it stopped, and slumped into her lap.

"Have you ever loved me?" she whispered—a genuine whisper that hit me in the heart.

"I have idolized you..." I said and she grasped my hand hard, again.

"Loved me, have you ever..." she whispered, a tear now forming in her right eye.

"Of course, mother. I still do. I am just afraid." I whispered, too.

"Afraid of me?" she said, looking wounded.

"No, afraid of not being like you."

Her eyes darted towards me, and a tear fell—I reached out with an embroidered hankie, at last useful.

"But I am not like you. I do not know what I am like. All I know is that I want... I *need*... to venture out into the world. Maybe I am like father in that way."

She swallowed. I stroked her hand as if she were a baby. I tried to remember a time she had done this to me, when I was very young, and recalled her singing a lullaby, too.

I hummed the lullaby and she held in a sob.

"I'm sorry," she said, the diamond dust having fallen from her face—into my eyes.

Cold as Hell

It's cold as hell. I thought it was going to be hot so I didn't bring any warm clothes.

I think this is how it works. You spend your whole life being told it's gonna be hot in hell, then you get here and you freeze your fucking ass off!

That's just cruel!

Right now I'd commit a sin just to get a little match, or a space heater. But no. I think my toes are gonna fall off.

This is freezer *burn,* that's it. That's why they were confused. It was probably some kind of terrible translation error from ancient Turmeric of whatever the fucking language was.

Fucking bullshit.

If I'd known this, then before I drove my Camry off the cliff I would have been wearing a parka and a ski hat and ski boots! Not a sleeveless shirt, flip flops and super cute short shorts.

I knew I'd go to hell, I knew that was gonna happen. And not because I drove off the cliff, either. I did plenty of things in my life which made sure I'd go to hell, so I figured, "why should I suffer on earth when I can go right to hell and suffer, I'll roast for a little while and it'll all be over with."

I didn't think I'd be here for eternity anyway, because I believe in Karma, which is why I think I'm in hell, because I generated a lot of bad Karma, but I also think I'll be back—I'll be back.

Maybe what happens is... oh, god, my little pinkie is blue... maybe as each appendage freezes and falls off and then there's nothing left of you, maybe that's when you get to start over, after having learned a valuable lesson, which is to wear thermal underwear.

Next time I go back, and there *will* be a next time, I know there will be a next time just like I knew I was coming to hell only I didn't know it would be frozen, so who knows... next time maybe I'll come back to earth... I could be a grape and come back as Chardonnay.

Fuck, I really don't know how it works. Just like I knew I was coming to hell and I did but I didn't know how it worked.

God, I wonder what I'll come back as. If we're thinking about Karma then I'd probably come back as a man to make up for all the crap I did to men, like Lance, my last fiancee.

He was a nice guy. OK, who am I kidding? He was a boring twat, but he said he liked my hair and my hair was very important to me. Thank God (I said "God" and nothing bad happened!) I have this hair. It's keeping my head warm, though I don't think the cold is good for the split ends. But in the end, it doesn't matter, right? Ha. Ha. Ha.

Eventually I'm gonna get reborn as someone else... That's what I always thought. God, now I'm afraid it's gonna be someTHING else. Seriously. Like I'll come back as a mink, which would be a real problem since I loved mink coats. See, maybe that's the Karma, I'll get skinned and turned into a cheap Czechoslovakian coat. That'd serve me right, wouldn't it?

But, maybe it'd be nice—can you imagine, having all that fur, feeling that sultry softness all the time? Having that lovely mink-y smell? Maybe I wouldn't mind coming back as a mink.

OH! My god! My feet hurt so much. It's like someone is sticking pins and needles into my feet. I don't know, I don't know, I'll get frostbite, my feet will fall off and then I won't even be able to stand up. If I can't stand up, then I'll freeze faster, so maybe that's what I should go for. Maybe I should go for the frozen foot fall over. Maybe I should just fall over. Oh, crap, that doesn't work, because I can't move.

Well. Huh. Nobody tells you what hell is really like. It's hell! You're fucking freezing and you're fucking frozen!

So... it's the opposite of what you think it's gonna be. I thought it would be hot, it's cold. I thought I'd come back as a person so maybe I would come back as a... oh, yeah, a man.

I know it. I'm pretty damned sure I'll come back as a man. Of course it may not be a male human, it may be a male fish or something, like one of those male fish that has to hold the eggs and have the babies. I don't remember what kind of fish that is.

I never wanted to have babies, so that's what will happen, I'll be a man and have to have babies. Jesus Fucking J. Christ, it's the worst of all things.

I'm pretty sure, right now, if I just itched my nose it would fall off my face, I'm pretty sure of that but I can't touch it so I don't know.

I'm just gonna be frozen here worrying about coming back as a man who has to have babies.

Ugh. This hell place is devious.

What the fuck. What. The. Bloody. Fuck. I can smell hot chocolate. I CAN SMELL HOT CHOCOLATE OUT THERE, DEMONS!

It's one torment after another. I mean I can smell the warmed milk and I can feel, oh, a tiny little bit of steam on my cheek, oh, that was so nice! I can even smell the marshmallows!

Maybe someone's gonna bring it to me. Maybe there's someone nice in hell and they're gonna take pity on me because it's not like I killed someone or something, I didn't kill anybody... except minks.

And I had an abortion, but that didn't count, they weren't born, they weren't a person, I believe that. I know it's true, besides, the father was a gay Mormon and it was not gonna end well. I did everybody a favor— hear that? It was not going to end well, demons!

That's not what they're holding against me, I'm pretty sure. But they should give you a list. When you get down here they should give you a list and say, "Look, here are all the ways you fucked up. Read the list and think about it when you're freezing your fucking ass off so when you go back next time you'll go, 'oh, not gonna make those mistakes again!'"

But, no. No. It's not like a correctional facility, they're not correcting anything here. The two times I went to a correctional facility it wasn't even called that, it was just called a jail and just overnight till my pimp could get me out.

But I'm not in hell for that, either, I'm telling you, I'm not. I was providing a service, nobody was harmed in the making of that love except for some minks. So that isn't it.

I do think that when I stole Lance's Civic and emptied out his bank account and went to Costa Rica with his adopted brother, Juan Carlos, that that was bad. I knew it was bad when I was doing it.

But, Lance was boring and JC was... wait, he wasn't even his real brother! See, that's what I said, they weren't even related. Yes, JC was his brother but adopted so it didn't count.

So when we went to Costa Rica... Wait, OK, it was bad, yes, I see, it was bad, I'm learning.

Argh. I'm also learning that my jaw is frozen. If I'd had a frozen jaw all those years I was working I'd never have made a living. Wow, this hurts like a son of a bitch, which that gay Mormon baby would have been!

Pff.

I would scream, but I can't open my mouth. I can't even make grunting noises. No. If I couldn't have grunted when I was alive I also wouldn't have made a living, either. I was great at grunting, that was my kind of professional name, "the grunter" you know, some guys like that.

No, I wasn't nice to Lance. And when I was doing it I kind of sensed a pattern, because the six previous times I'd been engaged it was always to the wrong person.

But that wasn't ever my fault. That was the fault of their brothers who weren't interested in me—so I thought I could make them jealous by getting with their brothers.

It never did work.

I mean, even Lance's so-called brother, Juan Carlos, tried to trade me to a drug lord for a brick of cocaine. Drug lord laughed in his face and said, "For that thing? Not even worth a gram."

I would have been insulted but he said it in Spanish so I didn't know what he was saying until later when JC was apologizing to Lance on the phone and he told that story in English.

I totally understood, I totally understood, I think Juan Carlos felt bad, I felt bad. We made mistakes, we both made mistakes, you're human you make mistakes.

Hmm. Everything feels frozen solid. The pain is excruciating. Yet nothing is falling off me.

This is a problem. This is a problem because I could be like that prehistoric woman and she was frozen for, I don't know, a thousand years or whatever she was frozen for.

Now I'm gonna have to spend the whole time frozen and in agony? This is bullshit.

Oh, I know what I'll do to pass the time. I'll think about what it is I want to be reincarnated as, then just so I don't jinx it, I'll say I want to be the exact opposite of that.

So if I focus, really, really focus on wanting to be one of those male fish who's pregnant, then I'll come back as a female who's never pregnant.

I think I have a plan here, I think I have stumbled upon a very important plan and if I can remember this plan when I get back to earth... if I could somehow, I don't know, have a talk show or a popular magazine or something I could write about this so everybody would know how it works.

Then I would be rich and famous and then the right men would be attracted to me, and by the right men I mean like if they're identical twins, like Doug and Dave were, then the one who I'm really interested in, like Doug because there was something about the shape of his ears that was a lot sexier than Dave's, he'd be into me.

And while they were both basketball players I thought, Dave... Doug... oh, god, I'm confused about who was which. Oh, well, the one I wanted wasn't the one I got.

Then I'm crying out his name during sex and, yeah, it was a problem.

I don't want to be one of those male fish that has babies, I don't want to be one of those male fish that has babies, I don't want to be one of those male fish that has babies...

No, this is torment, too, because now all I can imagine is being one of those male fish that has babies.

I'm gonna think about lying on Venice beach in my string bikini and getting baked in the sun! See, I didn't have to worry about all that, "Oooh, you're gonna get skin cancer!" crap because I died before that happened, so it wasn't a problem.

So I'll imagine myself in the sun... Oh, god, now, that's making me... ouch... making me... ouch... making me tingle, I don't like that. Don't think about that...

I just wanna think about what it's gonna be like when I get back to earth.

I want to be a beautiful woman just like I was. You know, smart, sexy, and can wear one of those really tight dresses without Spanx or anything.

I always had a good body. I always liked my body—everything. Except that little bump in my nose I didn't like. I was gonna have that removed when I made enough money but I never did but nobody else minded, nobody even noticed.

I would ask every guy I was engaged to, "Are you disgusted by this horrible bump on my nose," and they'd go, "Tiffy, you cray cray, I don't see no bump on your nose, bitch," and I'd say, "you must, you must, it's huge and it must nauseate you," and they'd go, "No! Now show me your tits," and I'd show 'em my tits and we'd move on but I'd still be thinking about the bump in my nose.

OK.

So I wanna be pretty, sexy, smart... pretty much exactly like I was.

Oh. That makes me feel better. Just to be exactly like I was.

Wait. What? My nose just fell off!

Fuck yes!

Pearls

The sun hit me in the eyes as it did every morning. That is why I put my sleeping mat there—so I would wake with the dawn. As the seasons changed I moved the mat around the small whitewashed room, always following the sun.

I splashed water on myself from the bowl. Half a lemon floated in it and made the room, and myself, smell sweeter as I patted it on my face, chest, under my arms. I stood in the light, my eyes closed, feeling the warmth of the sun and the coolness of the water.

I put on my toga—it was getting threadbare. I needed a new one. Surely there was something I could trade with the weaver, perhaps it was time for his wife's birth anniversary and she would want a pair of earrings—yes—I will suggest that to him. I will take the earrings out of my own ears and offer them, but not my best ones. I will wear a pair I have made just to trade. Pearls. Small ones. Still, it had better be a very fine toga if I include pearls.

Ah, a pomegranate is ripe just outside my window! Best to remove the toga first, pomegranate juice stains.

So I sit, naked, on the warm stone floor, eating pomegranate. They look like rubies in the sunlight. I have always wanted to make jewelry that looks like pomegranate. It is, by far, the most beautiful fruit.

Yes, when I am done with my commissions that is what I will make. But not for the weaver's wife.

The pomegranate juice is sweet, it drips down my chin onto my chest. I was right to remove my toga. I watch the blood red juice run down my skin, and I think about the time when I had Melina to lick it off me.

How the sun would touch us together in the morning. We would make love in the light and heat and douse each other in lemon water

I thought this would last forever.

I was young and foolish and blinded by love.

But she married a rich senator for whom I had made a signet ring. All the love I put into my work, into the annealing of the gold, the carving of the carnelian—she would deliver for me when I sold to men. They would be too distracted by her beauty to find any fault with the work—not that there was—but people will find it even where it does not exist.

As I found fault with her, seeing small lines appear on her face. Noticing how the ebony of her eyes turned to petrified wood.

Then she delivered the signet ring and the senator wanted more. Being a senator he got it. He got her.

And now, the pomegranate juice runs down to my navel, like a tear from my heart.

I am still young enough, and as a goldsmith, I am successful and comfortable. I would be a fine catch for any woman. But any woman cannot be Melina. The women who have tried seemed like sea glass to her emerald. They saw in me not a man with a warm heart, but a man with gold. Unaware that for me, gold was a commodity. My alchemy was not making gold, but turning it into something else.

I walked down the steps and turned right past the Colonos—the sky was white with the sun. The sea was white with waves. My head was filled with the chatter of families in their homes, of tradesmen in their shops, of horses hooves and dogs underfoot.

The smells of tagenites and pine nuts roasting formed the taste of fall on my tongue.

I reached my shop, put the large key in the lock and opened the iron gate. I swung it wide, pulled back the curtain letting the sun warm the cold stone walls. The light brought the room to life, illuminating the gold which warmed the room.

I had deliveries today but I knew better than to send anyone I cared for. I had been using a milkmaid, pretty enough girl, but dumb so I had no interest in her.

Then a new idea came into my mind. I would ask Callias, the weaver, if his wife could deliver the jewel for me—for once her hand touched the gold, I knew that she would crave it the way all humans do. In return, yes, yes, pearls. Seed pearls, but pearls none the less.

I locked my gate and walked west several doorways to Callias' weaving shop. He did beautiful work, but then, he must, because our shops were on the royal road, and only the best artisans could be here by order of the emperor.

I gave him a hearty greeting—he was a big man. I always wished I was a big man but I was frail, like my father. I asked him if I could spare a few moments of his time. His hands fell silent at the loom, for as I well know, one cannot concentrate on craft and speak at the same time.

I intimated that I needed to speak with him about a private matter. I asked him if his wife, Cymone, could deliver something for me.

He understood the power of a beautiful woman and Cymone had been beautiful— once. He nodded and called for Cymone who had been sweeping.

I told her the name of the gentleman, Gallus Kallinos. She knew where he lived, as her husband had made him a toga not long before. She smiled, her teeth beautiful, like pearls, and I thought, "This might be how Melina looks today."

She took the ring and wrapped it in a small cloth of her husband's making. In her absence I spoke with Callias. I told him perhaps she needed earrings to celebrate her birth and that I would be glad to trade for a new toga.

He smiled wearily and said he was not sure he had the time as he was busy. His son was in the army in Crete and could not help him as he used to.

I don't know why, but I felt such sadness for him—so big, and yet so weak.

I told him I understood and that I would not bother him again with the request. I sent wishes that his son was fine and his fingers fleet.

I returned to my shop. Soon Cymone arrived with the money. I do not know what possessed me but I looked at her smile and I wanted to do something for her. Something that her huge, but hesitant husband could not.

I showed her a pair of earrings and told her that her teeth reminded me of these pearls and she should try them on.

She did, and her beauty overwhelmed me.

Her age did not matter. She had a vibrancy that made me want to have her.

The earrings, I said, were valuable, but she was priceless. I wanted her to have them because such beauty belonged together.

Her cheeks turned pink and I felt the heat from her skin.

I locked the gate and closed the drape, and she was mine.

I was transported back to when I was with Melina, and yet, it was different. It was sweeter, as if she needed me as much as I needed her.

When we were done, a tear fell from her eye like a moonstone. She whispered that she had not been touched or told her she was beautiful in many seasons.

She took the earrings off. She could not accept them. She placed them gently in my palm and said she would instead wear my words—more precious than pearls.

Better than Alive

L ee's brain was on the seat next to me in a plastic bag. I stopped hard for a red light and it almost slid onto the floor. I reached out, protectively, felt it shaking, gelatinous. Cold.

Yet it didn't make me sad because this is exactly what he wanted. It's what he told me he wanted. More than that, it's what I knew he wanted because I knew him better than anyone else.

I knew what he tasted like and I'd swallowed him. He called me "my little cannibal," when he was in my mouth, his seed becoming part of me.

"Everybody's a cannibal. Even vegans. We're all eating away at each other. Physically, but even more insidiously and nourishingly, metaphorically." He would talk like this for hours on end when he was really high, sometimes even when he wasn't. He'd go on about how the entire financial system was based on cannibalism.

He said that nothing tasted better than greed and I can vouch for that because when he was greediest is when he tasted his best. I'd be on my knees in front of him, lapping him up, draining every last drop in the service of his genius.

And he was a genius. A lot of people are called that today, but if you knew him, you knew that. He had vision and didn't let anything stop him—so he could do anything.

He would say, "Roman, there's a fine line between beauty and ugliness. I have to cross it to show people where it is and make them appreciate both sides of it. There's a fine line between life and death and we all have to cross it, but I will cross it soon to see its beauty."

I lay there, naked, listening to him breathe, and asked "Why? I want you here."

"You only want to be here to feed off me," he said, cruelly, trying to get me to go.

"I'm not a vampire," I said, obviously, and he looked disappointed. "I do what I do in service of you."

He knew it as he stroked my cheek and ran his finger along my lips. Then he sighed and said what he always said, "You're the most loving person I've ever met." Only he added something new, "And I hate you for it."

I was stunned. He looked at me with a dead stare, like the kind he had when he wore those black contacts during his shows. Then he was hiding his soul. Now I thought it was really him here with me. But was it?

I turned away, "How can you say that?"

I felt his warm breath on my neck as he whispered, "Because you make me *want* to stay."

It was, at once, so beautiful and so mean, like I was doing something awful to him by loving him. I couldn't stand it. I got out of bed and left. I couldn't spend the night, I just couldn't, because I knew what might happen and I wouldn't be part of it.

I went back to my flat where I hadn't been in weeks. The windows were closed and it was so hot and stuffy, I flung them open, took off all my clothes and stood in the window, trying to breathe.

I wanted to scream. But it was 3:00 AM and I didn't want to wake up the neighbors. Truth is, I didn't want to wake up myself. So I stood there, silently, feeling the night air ooze around me, making my skin crawl, hating myself the way he hated me.

Even if I made him *want* to stay, I couldn't *make* him stay. But then, nobody could ever make Lee do anything—One of the reasons why I considered it a personal triumph I could make him make jizz. I could *make* him, even when he didn't feel like it. I never told anyone—it was my private victory.

Even now I could still taste him. There was a drop of him on my goatee. I wanted to save it and put it in the freezer and clone him. I actually thought of that—that I had a drop of genius on me, not to mention what I'd had in me. It seemed like it would be a terrible waste just to let it go, but I knew that's what he wanted. So I took one last taste with my tongue and swallowed. At least he would always be part of me.

The next morning I heard the news that he'd hung himself. I didn't cry, because I knew it was what he wanted and I hadn't gotten in the way. The only thing that made me sad was realizing it wouldn't have mattered what I did.

I already knew that he was done. That he'd put on his last show, that he couldn't take it anymore. He wanted to be with his dead mum, more than he wanted to be with me. I resented it, but I understood it.

I visited him at the coroner and did what he'd asked me to. While nobody was looking, I lifted the top of his skull and removed his brain. Removed it from the skull which had played such a big part in his designs.

I hurried out, thinking I might be on camera. But I remembered him telling me they would never say anything because it would be too embarrassing for them.

I drove to his country house, Fairlight, where he kept his dogs, Sid and Nancy. They were always happy to see me. They ran towards me, barking. They couldn't have been happier.

I untied the plastic bag and let his brain slide onto the grass, glistening in the sun. They lunged at it, madly devouring him—just like he wanted.

He'd said, "Roman, the world has chewed me up and swallowed me, and that just makes me feel dead. But when Sid and Nancy do it, I'll feel much better than alive."

Sahara Evergreen

"I wouldn't be caught dead here!" I joked, standing in the cemetery on the wrong side of the tracks.

Ever since I'd been diagnosed with Stage IV liver cancer, I was traveling around to see where I wanted to spend eternity.

I knew only my body would be there—my spirit would go to... heaven, I assumed, or at least hoped, as I had led a good life.

But I had never lived in a good place, and so even if it was foolish, I wanted my body interred someplace nice with a view, not here in Missouri, certainly not in this cemetery so close to the Mississippi where it could flood and I might be washed away to God knows where.

So the trip began. I made a list of cemeteries from here to California where famous people were buried, because I assumed if they were buried there it must be a nice place. This was the first stop. I read somewhere that Mark Twain was buried here, and it certainly did nothing for me, but then of course he loved big muddy.

I drove west. Next stop Arizona. This cemetery looked particularly beautiful online, a lush green square in the middle of parched desert.

The list of the people buried here was quite impressive, ranging from celebrities such as Waylon Jennings, who I remembered as that ventriloquist with his doll "Madame," to poets like that man who wrote about the pelicans.

And mostly, TV and sporting stars who I had grown up with as a child. The idea of spending eternity next to Gayle Gordon from "The Lucy Show" so excited me that I could hardly sleep the night before my visit, even though I needed to rest before the drive!

Would this mean, perhaps, that my soul would have an entree to Lucille Ball in the afterlife? That I would hobnob with famous lady golfers and tennis players, the kind I had always so admired. Those independent women like Lucy who I tried to model myself after, which is why I never cared to marry and spent 35 years teaching 6th grade in St. Louis.

When I arrived at "El Amor de los Muertos" through beautiful gates made of giant boulders, it was like stepping into another world, from barren desert into a kind of eternal oasis!

I knew the entrance fee here was steep. To water the grass and keep the grounds must have been a monumental effort. And how eternally effortful simply to keep the sands from overcoming it. But I had no heirs, my house would be sold, I could afford the down payment, then my estate would go to pay in perpetuity for the tomb owners association.

It felt like paradise! Ah, the sun beating down on me, the heat pressing in on me. I took off my shoes and felt the hot grass between my toes. I tried to imagine how cool it would be six feet under.

There was a large fountain spewing water high into the air. A rippling pond with swans! How lovely it would be here in this desert oasis with celebrities and swans keeping me company.

I went to the sales office and met Mr. Allentuck. His appearance surprised me—he was not dressed morbidly like they were in the midwest. He was wearing white pants and shoes, with a pink and green plaid sport coat.

He showed me the pictures on the wall, explaining how the Dinah Shore memorial golf tournament was held here each spring. Part of the proceeds went to taking care of the grounds, and a different resident each year was designated as the final hole— bringing even more glory to their name!

I tingled at the thought of pro-am golfers putting above my head.

But then Mr. Allentuck said something that surprised me. He said he thought I would be happy to know that there were many people of the Jewish persuasion here.

I guess it was because of my last name, Goldstein, he thought I was a Jew, but I was not. I had been adopted by a widow, a Catholic who had been mistakenly married to a Jew at a very young age, but her devout parents did not believe in divorce so she remained morally and unhappily married for 40 years.

Mama was a staunch believer that the Jews had killed our savior, so the idea of being surrounded by savior-killers soured the experience.

I continued west.

That night, in the hotel lobby, I searched my guidebook for Christian cemeteries and was relieved to find one only an hour's drive outside of Tucson.

"Mercy Springs," a good, Christian name. And true to its Christian values, there were many crosses and not a single star of David.

But there were also no swans. No fountains. And Mr. Babbitt, the salesman, was dressed in a dark suit and seemed unnecessarily solemn after the colorful Mr. Allentuck.

When I asked if there were any memorial golf tournaments here, Mr. Babbitt gave me a shaming look that only added to the disappointment of knowing there was not one single celebrity interred here.

I could not hide my disappointment at this fact, to which Mr. Babbitt suggested I go to "El

Amor de los Muertos" as that might be more to my "taste."

I commented on the plethora of Jews there, to which he remarked that I would be hard-pressed to find a celebrity cemetery without them.

I kept this in mind on my way back to the motel where I searched for my next destination—right outside of Las Vegas and home to most of the Rat Pack, all good Christians except for Sammy Davis Jr. who also suffered from being a Negro, but I had always enjoyed their entertainment and could only imagine the witty repartee in the afterlife.

So, the idea of forgiveness entered me, as it should when life is coming to a close. I decided to forgive the entire Jewish race and arrived at the gates of "Sahara Evergreen."

As I expected, there were many monuments to golfers, singers, and comedians—but there, shining at the top of a small man-made hill, was a carved obsidian fedora on top of a shining marble bust of Ol' Blue Eyes, which, upon closer inspection, had eyes made of genuine Lapis Lazuli.

My mother had adored Ol' Blue Eyes. I was sure she would approve.

So I met with Dr. Decker, he was a doctor of theology. He explained that Sahara Evergreen was a non-denominational land of rest, that it discriminated against no one based on religion, just the way St. Peter discriminated against no one.

Suddenly, the feeling of warmth returned to my liver the way it hadn't felt since the 90s, and I knew, "This is home!"

Dr. Decker showed me a map and explained that while every space in the vicinity of Ol' Blue Eyes had long since been filled, they were just about to break ground on the Sinatrarium, a 12 story Carrara Marble columbarium shaped like a stack of records, and topped with a spire inspired by the Columbia Records building where Sinatra had made his famous recordings.

This shining edifice would overlook the grave of Ol Blue Eyes and his music would play 24 hours a day on an "eternal loop," starting with his earliest recordings with Tommy Dorsey all the way to his final recording, "L.A. is my Lady." Naturally it would highlight a seasonal selection of Christian classics such as "Rudolph the Red Nosed Reindeer" recorded especially for the Montgomery Ward department store.

The top three floors were already sold out for Sinatra's own friends and family, all of whom longed to be near him and would have otherwise been turned out due to the lack of real estate.

I felt my face flush and my hand reaching for my checkbook as he played a video artist's rendering of what it would be like to enter into the sunlit atrium and look up at the stained glass dome that featured two giant blue eyes through which the sunbeams landed.

As the sun moved across the heavens, that blue glow would take turns illuminating every part of that circle, so that I knew, one day, if I chose level 6, space 214 in the north east corner, that right around December 1, during the chill of winter, I would be warmed by the glow of Ol' Blue Eyes!

Goosebumps ran up my arms as if mama Goldstein was watching over me, guiding my hand to write the down payment check for $48,000.

I almost wished I could drop dead right then so that this would be my last memory, and I could spend eternity here without ever having to return to my dark little house on the east side.

But Dr. Decker informed me that ground was just being broken and it would be at least nine months before the first residents moved in. If I couldn't make it that long, they would temporarily inter me in the basement crypt where they had already started playing Sinatra.

And while that was all fine and good, somehow this made me decide that I needed to live for at least nine months so that I knew I was going directly into the Sinatrarium.

I drove home and got my affairs in order. I sold my little house. I said my final goodbyes. I made peace with the fact that I would be leaving this world, because my excitement was so great about entering the next.

I moved into the Capri Sands motel just a mile away from Sahara Evergreen. My life was filled with exciting shows of Cirque du Soleil and Garth Brooks. I feasted on the endless variety of buffets, and replaced my drab old clothes with colorful summer dresses.

I basked in the sun even though this was February and woke up each morning excited about what the day would bring.

Despite this, as each day passed I became ever weaker. The joy of my new life in this desert oasis was peppered with the tears of knowing that I wouldn't be alive to enjoy it.

Daniel Will-Harris

Daniel Will-Harris is a best-selling author of five novels and stage plays.

MoMA has called Daniel's work "truly unique."

His 9 books have sold over 300,000 copies. He has three produced feature film screenplays to his credit and has written over 600 short stories currently featured in his popular story podcast. He's also an award-winning designer of wristwatches.

He's developed plays with the Kennedy Center Playwriting Intensive, Naked Angels Theater, and The Actor's Centre in London.

To learn his "Write in the Now" writing practice, go to www.WriteInTheNow.com

You can see all his work and contact him here: www.will-harris.com

www.ingramcontent.com/pod-product-compliance
Lightning Source LLC
Chambersburg PA
CBHW021956170626
46808CB00001B/177